At the heart of Jeremy Page's collection of long, short and flash fiction is the eponymous novella, *London Calling*, a comic tour-de-force set in a 1980s squat. Other stories feature a woman who remains in bed due to *ennui*, murder in a crime bookshop, and all the small resentments of a marriage condensed into two paragraphs. These are stories for our strange, unsettling times.

Jeremy Page is the author of several collections of poems and, since 1983, editor of the bi-annual literary journal *The Frogmore Papers*. He has also written two plays: *Loving Psyche* and *Verrall of the White Hart*, which were performed in Bremen (2010) and Lewes (2014), respectively. He lives close to the South Downs in Sussex and is currently Director of the Centre for Language Studies at the University of Sussex.

In these clever, surprising stories, Page's delicately delineated fictional characters struggle with marital micro-aggressions, the pathos of loss, and the mythical significance of a can of Special Brew. These are fictions which explore, with admirable poetic compression and superb control of imagery, the nature of reality; seemingly innocuous 'realistic' situations rapidly slide into alarming surreality. Language and meaning should be fixed and stable, but aren't; miscommunication and misunderstanding cause the ground beneath characters' feet to tilt, often alarmingly, leaving the reader both satisfied and unsettled. These are stories for our strange, unsettling times.

Catherine Smith, Writer, author of *The Biting Point*

Richly comic and mischievous, *London Calling* is a tour de force told at an unflinchingly lively pace. Following the torments of young would-be poet Eustace Tutt, Jeremy Page has managed to write a novella which is at once funny, tender and unputdownable.

Jane Bailey, Novelist, author of *Lark Song*

If P.G. Wodehouse could have time-travelled to a 1980s squat, *London Calling* is the novella he might have written. It's impossible to read without a big smile on your face and bursts of loud laughter as Eustace Tutt, wannabe poet, encounters the naked German girls, nascent artist Gaz, drunken literary magazine editor O'Mahony, and drama student Amy, who looks like a young Julie Christie. This wholly delightful tale transports us to a vividly visualized 1981, and ought to be on prescription as an antidote to 21st century blues.

Maggie Butt, Poet and novelist, author (as Maggie Brookes) of *House of Dreams*

Not since Paul Pennyfeather was sent down from Oxford has a disgraced student made me laugh so much. Chucked out of university, Eustace Tutt finds himself in a London squat in the early 80s, complete with Berlin nudists, a wannabe artist, and reclusive chemically inclined Rodney. But it's a chance meeting on his train to the Smoke that will change things for him: Amy Wildsmith, budding actor, '*not actress*'. Eustace has two ambitions: become a published poet and lose his virginity by the age of 21. But with everything so stacked against him, will he make it? A comic evocation of grim times – brilliant!

John O'Donoghue, Poet, journalist and author of *Sectioned: A Life Interrupted*

Also by Jeremy Page

Bliss (Crabflower Pamphlets, 1989)

Secret Dormitories (Crabflower Pamphlets, 1993)

The Alternative Version (Frogmore Press, 2001)

In and Out of the Dark Wood (HappenStance Press, 2010)

The Cost of All Desire: after Catullus (Ashley Press, 2011)

Closing Time (Pindrop Press, 2014)

Stepping Back: Resubmission for the Ordinary Level Examination in Psychogeography (Frogmore Press, 2016)

If Not Now/Dacă nu Acum (Integral Contemporary Literature Press, Bucharest, 2017)

London Calling
and Other Stories

Jeremy Page

Cultured Llama Publishing

First published in 2018 by
Cultured Llama Publishing
www.culturedllama.co.uk

ISBN 978-1-9164128-1-1

Printed in Great Britain by Lightning Source UK Ltd

Cover design: Mark Holihan
Painting: 'Rimbaud 2', by Reginald Gray

Contents

London calling to the underworld
Come out of the cupboard, you boys and girls.

The Clash, *London Calling*

London Calling

Tutt.
Eustace Tutt.
Eustace Tiberius Tutt.

Was it the curse of this name – those names – that had brought him to this?

Eustace Tutt was not Arthur Rimbaud, long dead poet, seer, gun-runner; sometime *enfant terrible* of French letters, lover of Paul Verlaine, *poète maudit,* celebrated sufferer of a season in hell. Eustace Tutt was not, had never been, would never be Arthur Rimbaud, save in his wildest fantasies.

It was a fact, though, that the wildest fantasies preoccupied a disproportionate number of the waking moments of Eustace Tiberius Tutt, with the consequence that they came to seem more real and therefore less questionable than the rituals of his everyday existence as an unexceptional student at an unexceptional university in the North of England.

As the delusion took hold, Eustace gave up attending lectures and seminars. Whole days were devoted to his efforts to derange his senses. Eustace developed increasingly sophisticated and efficient methods for drying the banana skins he subsequently smoked in a clay pipe; snuff was snorted till his nose bled; pot upon pot of valerian tea was brewed and consumed; the woods that surrounded the campus were scoured for hallucinogenic fungi. In the manner of his hero, Eustace came to regard matters of personal hygiene as an unwelcome distraction. He began to smell.

And in due course, the inevitable came to pass. Eustace was invited to suggest reasons why he should not be summarily ejected from the seat of learning, but in truth could think of none and had little appetite to invent any. Eustace Tiberius Tutt, the first Tutt, as far as anyone was aware, to gain entry to any prestigious seat of learning, was ejected, thrown out, sent down. His sojourn had lasted less than ten weeks.

Would any of this have come to pass if his name had been, say, Tony Smith, or Christopher Thompson? Who can say?

The fact that Eustace Tutt, who, as a result of some accident of genealogy and family tradition, had been baptised Eustace Tiberius Tutt, and who was not, in any corner of the reality shared by the rest of humanity, the great French poet and seer Arthur Rimbaud, now found himself, at the age of twenty, insolvent and without hope or purpose.

Had there been any other option, Eustace would not have returned to the bosom of his family in the small town on the south coast where he had spent his formative years. And had he remembered to wash in the twenty-seven days prior to his departure from the seat of learning, he might have required fewer than the nineteen lifts he somehow succeeded in securing to get him home.

2

3 January 1981

On the morning of Saturday 3rd January 1981 Eustace Tutt was awoken by the ringing of the telephone in the sitting room of his parents' semi-detached house in the town of his birth. Why he was fully clothed on the sofa rather than naked or pyjamaed in his attic room two floors up was uncertain, though an excess of alcohol the night before might have played its part.

'What?' asked Eustace peremptorily, having crawled across the room, groped for the receiver and slammed it into his ear.

'It's me. Gaz.'

'And?'

'Dingo's moving out. Going to live in Glastonbury.'

Eustace rubbed his eyes; noticed it was light outside.

'What time is it?'

'I don't know … half eleven maybe? Twelve?'

'Jesus. So why have you phoned me on a Saturday morning – it *is* Saturday, isn't it? – to tell me about Dingo?'

Gaz sighed audibly at the end of the line.

'Of course it's fucking Saturday. And the reason I'm phoning is because Dingo moving to Glastonbury means there's a room free at the squat. And it's yours if you want it.'

'At the squat?' Eustace repeated stupidly.

'That's right. Bloomsbury.'

'Clerkenwell, isn't it?'

'Bloomsbury.'

'Clerkenwell.'

'All right, Bloomsbury/Clerkenwell border. Who gives a toss anyway? Do you want it?'

'Which room is it?'

'Dingo's room, of course. In the basement.'

Eustace considered briefly. Clerkenwell was hardly Saint Germain des Prés. Regrettably, though, no-one was offering him free accommodation in Saint Germain des Prés.

'I'll take it.'

'Thank Christ for that,' said Gaz. 'When are you coming up?'

Much to his surprise and through the fug that seemed somehow to be clouding his brain this Saturday morning, Eustace felt a surge of excitement at the prospect of escaping the coastal town and relocating to the Metropolis.

'When's Dingo leaving?'

'Today. He's packing now. Look, Tutty, this is my last 10p. The pips are going to go in a minute.'

'Don't call me Tutty,' said Eustace automatically. 'I'll come up this afternoon. Can you meet me at Charing Cross? Five o'clock?'

But the pips so accurately forecast by Gaz duly intruded, and Eustace was left in ignorance of whether Gaz would be there to meet him or not.

He was suddenly aware that he had a very bad headache, possibly a hangover. Too much Bass at the Dog and Trumpet could have this effect, he'd previously noted. Looking at his feet, he was relieved to see that he had at least taken his shoes off. He cursed the daylight and made his way to the kitchen in search of an analgesic.

He chose the smoking compartment, as he always did. Explaining his sudden departure to the parents had taken considerably longer than he'd imagined and he was in need of a cigarette.

'But what are you going to *do*?' his father had wanted to know.

'Are there any cooking facilities in this *squat*?' had been his mother's concern.

To be fair, neither of them had really had time to come to terms with their son's removal from the seat of learning where he had allegedly been reading for a degree in

Modern European Languages and Literature. ('But what did you do for them to kick you out?' from his father. 'Did you feel out of place among all those academic types?' from his mother.)

And what he did not say was this: 'I discovered the work of the great French poet and seer, Arthur Rimbaud, and inspired by his example, I embarked upon a life of such utter dissolution that the thought of attending a lecture or producing an essay quite literally ceased to occur to me. Instead I experienced a *dérèglement de tous les sens,* and decided that I would become a poet. ' In fact, in response to their questions he'd said nothing at all, just shrugged his shoulders helplessly.

'Thank God your grandmother never lived to see it,' said his father.

'Thank God,' Eustace agreed with feeling.

And now, as he removed a cigarette from his packet of (ten) Guards, he became aware that the woman sitting opposite him – who, he could not help but notice, bore an astonishing resemblance to the young Julie Christie – was staring at him in what seemed to be a hostile fashion. Automatically he looked at the window to check he hadn't chosen a no smoking compartment in error, and saw to his relief that he hadn't.

'I'm sorry?' he began inquiringly.

'What for?'

'Would you prefer me not to smoke?'

'It's a free country,' she returned, 'and as far as I can see this is a smoking compartment.'

Eustace struck a Swan Vesta and lit his cigarette.

'Mind you, I wouldn't smoke one of those if you paid me,' she went on unbidden.

'I wasn't planning to,' Eustace assured her. 'Pay you, I mean.'

'Good,' she said, taking a packet of (ten) untipped Woodbines from her bag. 'Who are you anyway?'

'Eustace. Eustace Tutt,' he replied, holding out a hand across the carriage. After a moment's hesitation she leaned forward and shook it.

'I'm Amy Wildsmith. You don't exactly travel light, Eustace Tutt, do you?' She extracted a Woodbine and lit up.

'I'm moving to London,' said Eustace, wondering in passing why he was quite so willing to dance to this presumptuous young woman's tune. She raised an eyebrow.

'For what purpose?' she demanded to know.

'For no purpose at all,' replied Eustace without hesitation. 'I'm not very big on 'purpose'. As such.'

'Hmm,' said Amy Wildsmith, regarding him quizzically. 'These are difficult times to have the luxury of "not being big on purpose". Does that make you a man of means?'

Eustace snorted. 'My mother gave me my train fare and my father lent me twenty quid. And before they did that I had 62p in my pocket.'

'Mummy and Daddy to the rescue, then,' she remarked tartly. 'Do they always bail you out?'

'It's been known,' said Eustace defensively.

They sat in silence while the train pulled into a station. Several passengers looked into the compartment but decided against joining them. For his part, Eustace continued to wonder why he was bothering to engage in any further discussion. (This may have been due, in part, to her aforementioned resemblance to the young Julie Christie – circa 1965, *Doctor Zhivago* vintage.)

'Are you going all the way to London?' he ventured eventually.

'Yes, all the way,' she sighed, as if unimaginably bored. 'And then some.'

'Oh?'

'Crouch End,' she explained. 'N8. Miles from anywhere. At least two tubes, then a bus. Takes for ever.'

'Why do you live there?'

'It's where I study,' she returned in a scathing tone, as if the question had been unconscionably stupid. 'Drama. I'm going to be an actor.'

'An actress, surely?' Eustace could not stop himself suggesting.

'No, an actor. Do keep up, Eustace Tutt. It's 1981, not the Dark Ages.'

At that she stubbed out the remains of her Woodbine in the ashtray and extracted a book from her bag: *An Actor Prepares*. Stanislavski. She opened this with a flourish, communicating wordlessly that, from now on, she was not to be disturbed. Eustace closed his eyes, remembering his hangover, and promptly fell asleep. Whether he was disturbed at all by the frequent sardonic snorts from his companion as she read the work of the Great Russian is unrecorded. As is her reaction to the very loud snore he produced, as if from nowhere, as the train pulled into Waterloo East.

At Charing Cross she woke him up.

'We're here,' she announced. 'Big city, bright lights. I assume you were planning to get off, not make the return journey?'

Eustace came to with a start. The journey had taken one hour and forty-three minutes (or thereabouts), and he had been in a deep sleep since Ashford.

'Well?' she went on.

Eustace struggled to his feet.

'I'll give you a hand,' she said, as if in despair. 'God knows how you ever got to the station with all this luggage.'

Eustace decided against confessing that his father had driven him. They got off the train and made for the station concourse, Amy with a suitcase in each hand (both Eustace's) and a bag (hers) over her shoulder, Eustace with a kit bag in one hand and a rolled-up sleeping bag in the other.

Gaz was waiting for Eustace beyond the gate. Taller than Eustace, and even thinner, he had shoulder-length hair of indeterminate hue and was wearing an overcoat several sizes too large for him.

'Whoever's that?' Amy demanded.

'That's Gaz,' Eustace said, then, as if in explanation, 'he's an artist.'

'Oh, an artist,' repeated Amy, the quotation marks around the noun both loud and deeply ironic. 'Of the conceptual variety?' Though notionally a question, this was said in such a way as to establish that no answer was expected.

They presented their tickets – Eustace not without some difficulty, having forgotten that he'd placed his inside his pack of Guards for safe keeping – and emerged onto the concourse.

'Tutty, you old bugger!' said Gaz, advancing enthusiastically.

'Don't call me Tutty,' said Eustace automatically.

'And who's this?' Gaz continued with interest.

'Amy Wildsmith,' said Amy, depositing her travelling companion's suitcases on the ground and extending a hand, which Gaz shook warmly. 'I'm very pleased to meet you. I understand you're an artist. I hope you'll be a very successful one. But I have to go, I'm afraid. I have a long journey ahead of me.'

Gaz was staring at her with his mouth open. 'Has anyone ever told you you look just like–'

'Julie Christie. Yes, it happens all the time,' said Amy, as if looking like Julie Christie were the most normal thing in the world. She turned to Eustace.

'Give me your hand, Eustace Tutt.'

Without pausing to reflect, he did as he was bidden. Amy took a pen from her coat pocket and wrote seven digits on his hand: 341 3296.

'You can phone me if you like,' she said. 'Good-bye.'

And with that she was gone. Eustace and Gaz looked on in consternation as she sauntered off in the direction of the underground, lighting a Woodbine with a Clipper lighter as she went.

Later that evening, Gaz and Eustace installed themselves in the public bar of the Earth and Stars, the nearest pub to the squat, and referred to by Gaz as his 'local'.

'So what do you think of your new place?' he asked Eustace.

Eustace thought long and hard before answering. From the outside it was indistinguishable from the twenty-odd other houses in its terrace, all part of a late Victorian development that accounted for several neighbouring streets. The house was tall and thin, built from tawny grey London stock brick. There was a semi-basement that would constitute Eustace's quarters and three storeys above, with an extra room on each half-landing. The front garden was tiny, but there was a larger space at the rear, albeit in the form of an unprepossessing yard. In fact, the state of the squat had proved to be a pleasant surprise. It was a solid Victorian terraced house of the sort to be found in street after street in certain London postcodes. True, the paintwork was in need of attention everywhere except the kitchen and bathroom, and there was a marked lack of rugs or carpet. But the place was reasonably clean, and the absence of clutter gave it an air of relative tidiness. Gas, electricity and water all seemed to work, and what furniture there was looked clean if rather superannuated, as if it might have been rescued from a skip and then subjected to vigorous scrubbing.

'Not exactly the lap of luxury, is it?'

'Well, what do you expect for free?'

'I suppose. Who else is living there now, anyway?'

'There's just me, Hilde and Hanne, and then Rodney on the top floor.'

Eustace drank greedily from his pint of Guinness and lit a cigarette.

'Who are Hilde and Hanne?' he asked.

'Hildegard and Hannelore, to give them their proper names,' said Gaz. 'They're from Berlin.'

'What do they do?'

Gaz appeared perplexed by the question. Eustace caught himself thinking: that's what my father would have asked.

'Do?' repeated Gaz.

'Yeh, do,' said Eustace, 'you know, as in *to be is to do*.'

'Well, not much, I suppose,' Gaz replied eventually, having apparently given the matter considerable thought. 'I mean, they do a bit of life modelling. Hanne works behind the bar here when they're short-staffed. Otherwise they just kind of ... hang out.'

'Hang out?'

'Yeh. Oh,' he added as an afterthought, 'and they're often naked. You know, Germans and all that.'

Eustace was about to repeat the word 'naked' but stopped himself. He had a sudden insight into the nature of this dialogue with Gaz, and it somehow appalled him.

'Right,' he said, 'and the other one? Roderick, was it?'

'Rodney,' Gaz corrected him. 'Bit of a man of mystery, really. Hardly ever comes down from the top floor, and when he does he mostly doesn't speak. Just ... you know ... watches.'

'Watches?' (Damn, he was doing it again. Was there any virtue in mindless repetition?)

'Yeh, you know, doesn't really join in. Participate. It's like he's an audience.'

'An audience to what?'

'Conversations. Well, anything, really. He watched me doing the washing-up a couple of days ago.'

'He didn't help at all?'

'No. He did pick up a tea-cloth and I thought he was

going to dry, but he just put it down again.'

'Sounds like quite a character,' Eustace remarked sardonically.

'Oh, he's that all right,' Gaz agreed enthusiastically. 'I forgot to mention: he's supposed to be doing a PhD. On Ouspensky.'

'Ouspensky?'

'Russian esotericist. Disciple of Gurdjieff.'

'Sounds interesting.'

'Ouspensky?'

'Rodney.'

'Hard to tell,' said Gaz thoughtfully. 'He's mostly absent, and when he isn't he never speaks.'

7 January

It was to be several days before Eustace made the acquaintance of the Germans, who were, it seemed, away somewhere. When it occurred, his first encounter with Hildegard and Hannelore disconcerted him more than a little because he'd quite forgotten Gaz's warning about their habit of walking around the house unencumbered by clothes. On the Tuesday evening he came upon them at the kitchen table, apparently running a bath in the adjacent bathroom, both completely naked apart from the flip-flops on their feet. Having spent most of the day in the basement doing very little, Eustace blinked stupidly in the sudden light of the kitchen, his gaze travelling from the thin blonde one with very small breasts at the head of the table to the buxom redhead at her side.

'Are you Tutty?' asked the blonde, apparently unperturbed by his arrival. Eustace found himself staring foolishly at her nipples as he answered.

'Yes. I mean, no. That's to say, I'm Eustace. Eustace Tutt.'

The redhead stood up. Eustace noted with alarm that she was slightly taller than him, even in her flip-flops. She held out a hand.

'Hannelore. Pleased to meet you.'

'Likewise,' said Eustace, taking her hand, and trying not to look at her breasts.

'And I'm Hildegard,' said the blonde, standing up and extending her hand. 'You don't need a piss, do you? Only we're going to have a bath and we like to take our time.'

It was indeed in order to have a piss (as Hildegard so elegantly phrased it in her – to Eustace – perfectly charming German accent) that he had come upstairs, but for some reason or other he found himself responding in the negative, and thus resigned himself to forty-eight minutes of increasing discomfort.

When they emerged with towels around their heads, but otherwise unadorned, Hannelore fixed him with an uncompromising stare.

'We've left the water for you, Eustace,' she said.

'We thought maybe it has been a while since your last bath,' said Hildegard helpfully. 'There's plenty of soap.'

Eustace opened his mouth, but no words emerged.

'A long soak,' Hannelore recommended, patting him gently on the shoulder as she passed. When they'd gone, Eustace lifted his arm and quietly sniffed his armpit. It occurred to him that his last bath was a distant memory.

16 January

He had been in London for the best part of a fortnight when he first broached the subject of a possible loan with Gaz. While only the most generous of spirits could have accused him of exerting himself unduly in that time, it was true that he had managed to register here as a person without employment, and had even contacted the relevant authorities in the coastal town to notify them of his change of address. He had also taken a desultory wander around the local Job Centre before concluding (without obvious reluctance) that there was little here that his own (highly individual) attributes equipped him for. His first London Giro had yet to arrive and, despite his best efforts to restrict the number of Guards he smoked to no more than five a day and the number of pints of Bass he supped to no more than four a night (despite the generosity of Hanne in topping up his pint glass for free when the landlord's attention was elsewhere on the nights when she worked behind the bar at the Earth and Stars), funds had inevitably dwindled, and Eustace now found himself down to his last 25p.

So it was that on the Friday evening he forced himself to knock on the door of the large room that occupied much of the ground floor, and served both as Gaz's studio and as his bedroom.

'Yes?'

Eustace took this for an invitation to enter, but did so tentatively. Gaz stood at an easel, a brush in his left hand, a palette in his right. On the mattress on the floor that did service as his bed lay Hilde, naked but for a bottle green beret, reclining in leisurely fashion on her back, her right leg bent at the knee almost, but not quite, obscuring her bush, which (Eustace could not help noticing), unlike the hair on her head, was dark brown.

'Oh, hello Tutty,' said Gaz, glancing away from his canvas for a split second. 'How's it going?'

'Don't call me Tutty,' muttered Eustace, coming further into the room. He didn't consider it polite to remark that he could see no connection between the thin, wan German on the mattress and the splashes of white, brown and (okay) bottle green on the canvas.

'Oh sorry,' he went on. 'Didn't realise you were working.'

'I'm always working, me,' returned Gaz. 'If I'm not painting or sculpting, I'm looking.'

'Or cleaning floors at the hospital!' Hilde added tartly from the bed, without moving.

'Yes, or that,' Gaz agreed reluctantly. 'Well, you've got to earn a crust, haven't you?

How can we help?'

'Well, the thing is…'

'You need a loan,' suggested Gaz helpfully. 'Your Giro hasn't arrived and you're skint.'

'More or less,' Eustace agreed. 'Although I do have 25p.'

'Have you found a job yet?' asked Hilde, again without moving.

'Not yet,' Eustace admitted.

'Why not?' she demanded.

'It's tough out there,' said Eustace defensively. 'Too many people chasing too few jobs.'

'Hmm.' The German appeared less than convinced.

'I could ask at the hospital, see if there's anything going,' Gaz offered.

'What as?' asked Eustace sarcastically. 'Brain surgeon?'

Gaz put down his brush.

'Porter. Or domestic maybe. Like me.'

'Cleaning floors?'

'Not just floors. Baths, sinks. It can be quite interesting, actually…'

Eustace reflected. The prospect did not appeal.

'Beggars can't be choosers,' opined the prone and naked German. 'I'll lend you £20 till next Friday if you agree to go to the hospital and ask for a job. If you don't pay me back next Friday, I'll charge interest at 20% a week, rising to 50% if you haven't paid me back by the end of the month.'

Eustace looked helplessly at Gaz.

'You won't get a better offer,' the artist advised him. 'I'm skint and I don't get paid again until Friday.'

Eustace sighed.

'All right,' he said. 'It's a deal. Can I have it now?'

Still the German did not move.

'Do I look like the kind of woman who could keep a wad of notes between her tits? For that you would need Hannelore. I'll bring it to your room when Gaz has finished with me. Two crisp brown ten pound notes in a brown envelope.'

'No need for an envelope,' said Eustace.

'There's every need for an envelope,' Hilde responded sternly. 'I'll see you later.'

Gaz looked at Eustace and shrugged. Chastened, Eustace withdrew.

Later, having taken delivery of his brown envelope and its brown contents, Eustace made straight for the shop on Grays Inn Road that he had adopted as his supplier of Guards. It was a newsagent/tobacconist's that had not seen the benefit of any obvious redecoration since the '50s, and its sole proprietor, and permanent fixture behind the counter, was a woman of Icelandic origin and diminutive stature known as Mrs Rasmussen (though there was speculation in some quarters that this might not be her real name). To his considerable surprise, Mrs Rasmussen had been prepared on only the third day of their acquaintance to let Eustace have ten Guards on tick, and as a result, he felt a deep moral obligation to put whatever business he could her way. For her part, she seemed to have developed an inexplicable affection for the pale young man who had moved into the squat round the corner.

'Eustace!' she exclaimed whenever he entered her shop, as if he were some long lost friend. 'How nice to see you.'

'Evening, Mrs R,' he returned jovially (having affected a jovial air in the course of his earlier efforts to obtain tick, he was reluctant now to reveal his true disposition – which was infinitely darker and more gloomy). 'Had a good day?'

'Not bad, not bad,' she conceded, stroking her vast tabby cat, which lay across the *Evening News* and *Evening Standards* on the counter. It was a curious fact that the cat and his owner shared an identical hair colour.

'I'd like to settle my account, please,' Eustace continued grandly, 'and I'll have ten more of the best, please.'

'Certainly.' Mrs Rasmussen took the proffered ten pound note, rang up the cost of twenty Guards on her ancient till, and handed Eustace his cigarettes and his change. 'Any luck with finding a job, dear?' she enquired.

'Things are looking up,' Eustace assured her. 'I've got an interview at the hospital next week. Well, I may have.'

'That's wonderful news!' said Mrs Rasmussen, clapping her hands and startling the cat out of its slumber in a way that Eustace could not help finding disproportionate to the news he'd vouchsafed. 'I'll keep my fingers knotted for you!'

'Thanks,' said Eustace. 'I'll let you know what happens. And thanks, you know … about the cigarettes.'

'You're welcome,' Mrs Rasmussen beamed. 'It's a hard life for you young people with that Mrs *Thatcher* (she almost spat the name's two syllables out) in Downing Street. Have a good weekend, dear.'

'And you.' Eustace lit a cigarette and left the shop.

17 January

'How long would it take to walk to Camden from here?' asked Eustace. It was Saturday morning and he was sitting at the kitchen table sharing a pot of PG Tips with Gaz and Hildegard. Gaz was wearing a heavy quilted purple dressing gown while Hilde was wearing only her bottle green beret.

'Dunno,' said Gaz. 'Three quarters of an hour maybe? Fifty minutes? Why?'

Eustace reached for a cigarette.

'Thought I might go and have a look at Rimbaud's house. He lived there with Verlaine for a while, you know. About a hundred years ago.'

'Really.' The downward trajectory of Gaz's intonation

betrayed a marked lack of interest. Hildegard, contrariwise, appeared excited by this information.

'What did they do there?' she wanted to know. 'Devote themselves to the muse?'

'Well, Verlaine once attacked Rimbaud with a fish, apparently,' said Eustace. 'It's in the biography I read.'

'Interesting choice of weapon,' Gaz observed, suddenly keen to know more. 'A fish, eh?'

'Yes, hit him round the face with it.'

'A dead fish, I imagine,' Hilde remarked. 'Or at least, dead after the attack.'

Eustace was still in the process of making the acquaintance of the German sense of humour. He smiled doubtfully.

'Does anyone fancy walking to Camden with me?' he asked.

'Sorry, I've got work to do,' said Gaz, adding, in a distracted tone, 'conceptual.'

'I'll come,' Hilde offered. 'Give me ten minutes.'

She got up from the table and left the kitchen. Did Eustace imagine that she sniffed discreetly as she passed him? Either way, he automatically followed her with his eyes while noting that Gaz's interest was insufficient to tempt his away from the crossword.

'Don't they ever wear any clothes?' he wondered aloud.

'It's against their religion,' said Gaz. 'You'll get used to it. I don't even notice it any more. Most of the time.'

Hilde returned in precisely ten minutes. She was still wearing her green beret, but its significance was somewhat diminished now that she was also wearing a bulky duffle coat and a pair of Birkenstocks. Eustace supposed there were some other garments involved beneath the coat, but allowed himself to briefly enjoy the thought that there might not be.

'Shall we go, Eustace?' she asked brightly.

They went. It wasn't an especially pleasant walk. Gray's

Inn Road seemed interminable, Somerstown particularly charmless. As they reached Mornington Crescent it started to drizzle and continued relentlessly. Eustace was grateful for the company of the German, who kept him entertained and only mentioned Nietzsche twice. They found the house without difficulty and stood on the pavement looking up at it.

'It's amazing to think that they actually lived here,' said Hilde. 'Such an ordinary looking house, such extraordinary residents.'

Eustace's thoughts had strayed more prosaically to Verlaine's assault on his young lover with a fish; the dead one.

'One day, Eustace, people will come to the squat to see the house where you lived,' said Hilde.

Eustace struggled and failed to convince himself that she was being serious, but the thought was such a delicious one that he allowed it to linger a while anyway.

'Very funny,' he remarked finally, fearful that she would think him deluded.

'I'm German,' she reminded him. 'If I was being funny, I would have to be able to explain the joke.'

Eustace considered this, decided it might constitute a compliment, of sorts, and lit a cigarette. They stood in the drizzle a little longer, looking at the great man's house, then found a café.

7 February
It was not until he had done all of the following that Eustace availed himself of the telephone box along the road from the squat to call the number he had been given by Amy Wildsmith on Charing Cross station:

- secured gainful employment as a cleaner of floors and lavatories at the hospital where Gaz fulfilled similar duties;
- purchased a second-hand bicycle of dubious provenance (but endowed with four Sturmey Archer gears) from a character of dubious provenance at Brick Lane

market for the sum of nine pounds and fifty pence (haggled down from the ten pounds initially – and in Eustace's considered opinion, optimistically – proposed);
- repaid the loan extracted in so businesslike a fashion from his disconcertingly German fellow squatter, Hildegard (albeit only by the expedient of negotiating another loan – of the interest-free variety was his sincere hope – from Gaz).

He noted with mild surprise as he inserted the requisite 2p piece into the phone apparatus that this was a moment he had anticipated keenly for some time (possibly from the very moment when Amy Wildsmith had written the numbers 341 3296 on his hand).

'341 3296, hello?'

'Hello. Is that Amy?'

'One moment.'

He heard the receiver put down, then, after a pause that could not be measured, Amy's voice.

'Yes?'

Eustace worked hard not to notice the lack of any obvious warmth or encouragement in her tone.

'It's Eustace. Eustace Tutt.'

There was silence.

'From the train,' he added helpfully.

'Eustace Tutt!' she managed somehow almost to snort his name. 'Well, I thought you must have fled the country. Or gone into hibernation. Or died.'

'No, none of the above,' Eustace assured her, affecting his jocular tone. 'Just, you know, getting myself sorted.'

(He noted at this point that the phone was demanding more funds, which occasioned a frantic searching of his coat pockets; happily, this culminated in the discovery of another 2p with seconds to spare.)

'Look, I was wondering,' he went on, 'if we could, I don't know, maybe go for a drink or something?'

'I'll meet you by the Clock Tower, Crouch End, 8 o'clock Thursday evening. Don't be late. I never wait. Life's too short.'

'8 o'clock, Thursday, Crouch End Clock Tower,' Eustace repeated dutifully. 'I'll be there.'

'Good-bye, Eustace Tutt.'

She hung up.

12–13 February

By the Thursday in question Eustace had commenced his employment as a cleaner of floors and lavatories at the hospital and had, for four consecutive mornings, arisen at the ungodly hour of 6.00 am to cycle eastwards through the freezing streets of the capital in the company of his oldest friend, Gaz. At Smithfield Market, they would dismount and wheel their bicycles through the surreal early morning spectacle that seemed to Eustace to feature every species of edible mammal and bird known to humankind, carved into a seemingly infinite variety of shapes, and illuminated by neon lights. The butchers, all of them huge and ruddy of complexion, paid Gaz and Eustace scant regard while, for his part, Eustace already thought nothing of finding himself suddenly confronted by a vanload of pigs' heads.

At the hospital, he had been assigned to the same supervisor as Gaz, a formidable flaxen-haired woman of impressive stature and improbable cleavage in her late forties (or thereabouts), by the name of Mrs Clout.

'You must be Tutty,' she said on his first day, looking him up and down appraisingly.

'Eustace,' Eustace corrected her. 'Eustace Tutt.'

'Well, Tutty or Tutt,' she said, 'it's the renal ward for you today, so I hope you've got a strong stomach. Some of the specimens you'll see in that sluice would be enough to…'

'Specimens?' Eustace interrupted uncomprehendingly.

'Stool specimens,' Mrs Clout elaborated. 'You know, poo. Turds to you and me.'

'Oh,' said Eustace, 'I see.'

'It's what you might call a baptism by faeces.'

Eustace couldn't decide how much pleasure this was giving Mrs Clout, but it was clearly more than a little.

'Now run along, and I'll drop by in a while to see how you're getting on. The orderly will tell you where to find everything – ask for Bertha.'

She dismissed him with a wave of her hand, and Eustace was disconcerted to discover, moments later, that he was literally running along, albeit without any very clear idea of where he was going.

He had somehow endured four days of sweeping, mopping and scrubbing – four days to which he had already mentally assigned the label *my season in hell* after a similarly torturous period in the life of his great hero, Arthur Rimbaud – when, late on the Thursday afternoon in question, he walked from the squat to Kings Cross, took a Victoria Line train to Finsbury Park and boarded a W3 bus, which would, he was advised by Bertha, who had a sister in Hornsey, deliver him to Crouch End and the Clock Tower, where Amy Wildsmith had ordered him to meet her.

So clear had been her assertion that any lack of punctuality on his part would not be tolerated that he arrived a full hour, six minutes and thirty-nine seconds ahead of the appointed time of their meeting; and this despite the fact that the bus journey from Finsbury Park to the Broadway had seemed to take a good deal longer than was good for anyone.

Having established that Crouch End did not possess more than one clock tower – and, reluctant to rely exclusively on the evidence of his own eyes in this regard, he had felt compelled to enquire of someone he took to be local if there might, by any chance, be some other clock tower lurking mischievously at some remove from the Broadway (this resulting in a look of disbelief bordering on terror, followed by a hurried shake of the head) – Eustace set out to explore the environs, mindful that a wait of an hour might prove tiresome. It was not long (less than five minutes as the crow flies) or far (less than five hundred yards) before he came upon a vast, barn-like public house, which, in the absence of any obvious alternatives, he duly entered, installing himself at a table with a pint of Guinness and lighting a cigarette. He took a notebook and pen from the inside pocket of his overcoat and stared into space, waiting for inspiration to strike him.

He had been in this pose for some moments when he was indeed struck. But it was not inspiration that proved to be Eustace's assailant, but a wad of paper, which hit him in the forehead.

'Jesus, I'm sorry,' said a thickset bearded man with an Irish accent, stumbling towards him. (You'd have said he'd taken a drink or two.) 'I was aiming for the bin there.' He stooped to pick up the offending papers. 'These poems jointly and collectively constitute the biggest pile of shite it's been my misfortune to read in a long time. In fact, I'd say the bin's too good for them. I'm going to use them to wipe my arse. Now there's poetic justice.' He stuffed the offending pages into the pocket of his threadbare greatcoat and, without awaiting any invitation, seated himself at Eustace's table.

'Seamus O'Mahony,' he announced, holding out a hand for Eustace to shake and adding, lest there be any confusion, 'that's me. Not the author of that cack masquerading as poetry. That would be a young woman, I believe, a young woman by the name of Sue...' (he groped for a surname) 'oh, Sue something or other. On a par with the Bard himself, to hear some of them talk about her. Bollocks, I say, bollocks!'

Eustace took the proffered hand and shook it uncertainly.

'Eustace Tutt,' he said, adding, to his own subsequent surprise, 'poet.'

O'Mahony raised an eyebrow.

'A poet, is it?' he said thoughtfully, stroking his chin. 'And would the poet be able to spare a cigarette for a servant of poetry, who has unaccountably come out without his own?'

Despite faint feelings of foreboding Eustace offered his pack of Guards. O'Mahony took one of the two remaining cigarettes, which he lit with a lighter in the shape of a pistol. He inhaled deeply and with satisfaction.

'You, sir, have not only the soul of a poet but the manners of a gentleman. Though if I may say so, Guards are an odd choice of cigarette for a poet. I'd be thinking more Disque Bleu myself. Or Gauloises. I don't suppose you could see your way to purchasing me a pint of the dark stuff to keep yours company, could you? I could swear it was two five pound notes I had in my wallet when I came out, but whatever the facts of the matter I've only 18p left, and that's the truth.'

Eustace, of course, had had favours asked of him on numerous occasions since his arrival in the city, and had never experienced any difficulty in declining. Indeed he had cultivated a variety of ways of doing so, from affecting not to have heard to claiming abject poverty on his own behalf (frequently without recourse even to untruths). On this occasion, however, and again much to his subsequent surprise, he made obediently for the bar, returning with a pint of Guinness for his new companion.

'Slainte!' said O'Mahony, beaming, as he raised the glass to his lips and took a generous swig. 'Now tell me all about this poetry of yours, why don't you.'

The conversation that ensued was lengthy and increasingly incoherent in its nature. Eustace was, as may have been inferred, several pints behind O'Mahony, but as the evening wore on, an impartial observer would have struggled to say who was the more inebriated. It was not long short of nine o'clock when Eustace, at the bar and about to order yet another round, discovered that he was down to his last few pence. With this discovery came the realisation that he had missed his assignation with Amy Wildsmith at the Clock Tower, which should have taken place some fifty-five minutes previously; and that he had no way of paying for bus, tube or any other means of transport back to the squat. On the positive side, he had a new (unpaid) job as assistant editor of O'Mahony's poetry journal *Scripsi*, and the prospect that O'Mahony might one day consider some of his poems for possible publication in its pages.

What didn't happen that dark February night was this: Eustace did not experience a convivial evening in the company of the lovely Amy, in the course of which she recognised the qualities that set him apart from every other man she had known to date, decided to give herself to him unreservedly, invited him back to her flat and into her bed, where they undressed each other tenderly and made passionate love until daybreak.

What did happen was this: Eustace and O'Mahony staggered back to the latter's run-down Edwardian terraced house off Turnpike Lane, where O'Mahony made cheese on toast (Eustace's first solid food since noon) and produced a bottle of Powers, and both fell asleep in armchairs either side of the gas-fire in the sitting room. And neither stirred until the postman rang the doorbell shortly after nine the next morning, by which time it was much too late to think about going to work. Eustace's head ached and his pain, it seemed, was much greater than O'Mahony's. His season in hell had entered a whole new phase.

Late that afternoon Eustace was still feeling considerably less well than he would have wished as he nursed a mug of PG Tips in the kitchen at the squat. The Germans were out somewhere, there was no knowing whether Rodney was ensconced in his attic room or indeed in residence anywhere on the planet, and Eustace was almost enjoying the calm of the moment when it was unceremoniously shattered by the noisy return of Gaz.

'Jesus, Tutty, what happened to you?' were his first words. 'Ma Clout was livid. No-one to slop out the sluice on renal. Where have you been? In bed with the lovely Amy?'

Eustace regarded him malevolently. 'Don't call me Tutty.'

Gaz poured himself a mug of tea from the pot. 'Okay, okay,' he conceded. 'Reveal all.'

Eustace took a deep breath. 'I didn't see Amy, but I got a new job.'

'That's good,' said Gaz, ''cos Ma Clout is going to give you an official warning first thing Monday morning.'

'But it doesn't exactly involve getting paid or anything,' Eustace continued, 'so I won't be giving up the hospital. Not yet.'

'Then you'd better have a good story,' Gaz remarked, pulling up a chair. 'Why don't you tell me what really happened, then we'll turn it into fiction. Of the convincing variety.'

With some reluctance Eustace recounted the events of the previous evening. As he and Gaz had known each other since they were four, he didn't feel obliged to omit any of those details that made him appear most stupid and, as a result, the version vouchsafed to Gaz was more truthful than might have been expected.

'You wally,' was Gaz's judgment when he'd heard it all. 'Did you phone Amy?'

'No,' Eustace admitted.

'Do it,' said Gaz, 'now. The longer you leave it, the less chance she'll forgive you.'

'Why should I care if she forgives me?' asked Eustace, more for the hell of it than out of any need to ask his oldest friend the obvious.

'Don't be a wanker, Tutty,' said Gaz, good humouredly. 'I'll even lend you 2p to make the call before you claim you haven't got any change.'

'My head still hurts,' Eustace protested.

'And my heart bleeds,' countered Gaz. 'Now for fuck's sake go and phone her. The fresh air will do you good.'

'Amy?'

'Who's asking?'

'Eustace Tutt.'

'Eustace Tutt? Do I know a Eustace Tutt?'

'Look, Amy, I'm really sorry. I can't apologise enough. Really.'

(Pause.)

'Next you'll be telling me you met a man in a pub. Had a drink, then another. Didn't realise the time. Before you knew it, it was well after nine and you knew I'd be gone.'

'Yes, pretty much.'

(Loud guffaw.)

'Sorry?'

'That, Eustace Tutt, is pathetic. So pathetic it actually made me laugh. And I haven't had many laughs today. I'm almost tempted to give you a second chance.'

'That would be … very kind of you. I mean, yes, please do.'

'It would be wholly contrary to custom and practice.'

(Eustace was suddenly conscious that he didn't have another 2p and that call-time was finite.)

'Perhaps … in the circumstances…'

'Next Thursday. Same time, same place. And if you aren't there…'

'–?'

'I'll come and find you and cut your gonads off. With a blunt knife.'

The phone went dead.

14–15 February

It was quite by chance that Eustace discovered a significant public event was scheduled for the occasion of his twenty-first birthday, 29 July 1981: the future King of England would marry Lady Diana Spencer amid much pomp and ceremony at Westminster Abbey. Rodney had left a copy of the *Evening News* on the kitchen table at the squat, and while leafing through its pages Eustace had come across an article with the headline: *29 July 1981: the day a nation comes together in celebration.*

The sense of doom at his impending birthday, of which he had been dimly aware, was suddenly magnified to the power of ten. He would be twenty-one. By twenty-one his great hero Arthur Rimbaud had all but retired from poetry. By contrast, he, Eustace Tiberius Tutt, had yet to complete a poem, let alone publish one. (*Pace* Paul Valéry, he had, of course, abandoned several, but this thought provided scant comfort.)

Eustace stood confronted by his own failure. The danger that his life would continue to have as little meaning as it had had to date seemed suddenly very real. With the assistance of a mug of PG Tips and the last of his first pack of Gauloises, he resolved there and then that he would be a real poet by the age of twenty-one; or, at the very least, he would have created poems accepted for publication, whether by Seamus O'Mahony at *Scripsi* or elsewhere. And to that end he would spend the weekend engaging in the *dérèglement de tous les sens* that would facilitate the expression of his genius. He stubbed out his cigarette and summoned the courage to climb the stairs to the attic with a view to establishing what pharmaceutical assistance Rodney might be able to provide.

It proved to be a very long weekend. Much of it was spent by Eustace at his desk, awaiting inspiration. His senses were less deranged than he would have wished as a result of Rodney's failure (or refusal, who knows?) to open his door. The valerian tea-bags offered by the Germans had not produced quite the effect desired, despite their assurances. The infusion he had drunk on the Friday evening had sent him into a profound slumber, while the cup he'd started the day with on Saturday had done no more than make him feel slightly light-headed. Nevertheless, in the absence of any serious alternative, he had persisted, punctuating the time spent at his desk with regular visits to the kitchen to boil a kettle and make more. The weekend thus came to last rather longer than its allocation of hours, and proved to be a very strange one to boot.

By Sunday evening Eustace had produced the bare bones of a sonnet. He also found that he had vague recollections of events that might or might not have happened in the preceding two days.

Had he really found Gaz in bed with Hildegard and Hannelore in his studio? He couldn't be sure.

Had Mrs Rasmussen really confided that she'd been married three times, to an Irishman, a Dane and a fellow Icelander who drowned at sea? Eustace had no very clear idea.

And could it really be that Eustace, stirred by the spirit of Saint Valentine, had left the house in the middle of the night, made for the public phone box and rung Amy Wildsmith? Was it possible that he'd told her he really was a poet now and that he thought he loved her? That he'd never met anyone like her before in all his life?

Surely not.

16 February

However, Eustace had little cause to doubt the reality of his encounter with Mrs Clout the next morning.

'We missed you on Friday,' she began gently.

'Yes, I'm sorry,' muttered Eustace, who, since his mind had been on higher things, had given little thought to how he might explain his absence.

'Sick, were you?' she went on.

'Yes,' Eustace agreed gratefully. 'A stomach bug. Must have been something I ate.'

'Hung over more like,' Mrs Clout remarked tartly. 'And you didn't phone because…?'

'We don't have a phone where I live,' said Eustace unconvincingly (despite the fact that this was true), 'and my diarrhoea was so bad I couldn't make it to the phone box down the street.'

Mrs Clout did not trouble herself to give the impression that she believed the smallest portion of the guff she'd been offered in explanation.

'Consider yourself on a warning,' she said darkly. 'If it happens again you'll be out. Now get up to renal and clean that sluice.'

'Yes, Mrs Clout. Thank you, Mrs Clout,' muttered Eustace meekly, and walked briskly away until he was safely out of her line of vision. 'Old trout,' he added under his breath, as a sop to his pride.

'Look at this,' said O'Mahony. They were seated at the kitchen table of his house off Turnpike Lane, ploughing through a huge pile of manuscripts submitted to *Scripsi* by hopeful and aspiring poets. 'It's utter bollocks. 'Swansongs' she calls it. More like swan shite.'

Eustace took the manuscript and gave it a cursory glance. In truth he did not feel equipped to judge whether it had any merit, but felt it politic to agree.

'That's bad,' he said, shaking his head. 'That's really bad.'

'I'm glad you agree,' said O'Mahony. 'Send it back with the standard rejection note, would you?'

Fuelled by regular injections of Powers whiskey, they worked solidly for three hours, their reading punctuated by regular snorts of derision from the one or the other and the very occasional murmur of approval from O'Mahony.

'This isn't altogether shite,' he'd remark. 'We might think about publishing it, I suppose.'

For his part Eustace did not dare express approval of anything he read unless invited to do so by O'Mahony. The fear that he might mistakenly find some merit in work that was manifestly as shite as 'Swansongs' and the consequent and inevitable humiliation if he did so ensured that Eustace derided frequently and was careful never to praise or even intimate he'd found something that just might be worthy of publication. O'Mahony seemed happy for his new assistant to reject manuscript after manuscript, his mood becoming ever brighter the more rejection slips Eustace got through.

'We're going to make a grand team,' he said, shortly after ten o'clock, taking off his reading glasses. 'And you, Eustace, have earned a pint. We might even get a couple in before last orders.'

'I'm not sure,' Eustace began to protest feebly. 'I've got to be up for work at six. And I've got to cycle home. And we've had quite a lot of whiskey.'

'Nonsense,' said O'Mahony, dismissing his protests and putting on his coat. '*Scripsi* may not be able to pay you a wage for your labour – and God knows reading some of this shite is labour in anybody's books – but we can run to a pint or two. Now where did I put that fiver?'

To Eustace's surprise, O'Mahony located the note, which was pinned to a cork board next to the kitchen sink.

'Ah, there it is! Now come on, Eustace. What the devil are you waiting for?'

Eustace sighed, pulled on his coat and resigned himself to a night of little sleep. Perhaps a half bottle of Powers, a couple of pints and a bicycle ride through the chilly night air back to Clerkenwell could constitute a *dérèglement de tous les sens*? Perhaps he'd be so inspired that he'd spend the night at his desk penning a work of poetic genius.

17 February

He was rudely woken at six the next morning.

'Tutty! Come on, it's after six. You're going to be late.'

'Don't call me Tutty,' said Eustace automatically in his sleep. Gaz threw a shoe at his head.

'Just get up, you plonker. You're already on a warning.'

Eustace came to with a start. His basement room had thick black drapes at the window, through which, in any case, very little light would ever have succeeded in penetrating. He rubbed his eyes, put on his bedside light and reached for his Gauloises. Twenty minutes later he and Gaz were cycling through the early morning to the hospital.

'I've decided to go to art school,' Gaz announced. 'I'm not getting anywhere without the right contacts. I haven't sold a painting or anything else for months. It's getting me down.'

Eustace struggled with the very idea of conversation at this hour of the day, but felt obliged to show interest in view of the many favours Gaz had done him in recent months.

'Where are you thinking of going?' he dutifully asked as they approached High Holborn.

'I dunno. Goldsmiths maybe. If they'd have me. I gather they specialise in unlikely types like me.'

'So what's your plan?'

'Well, I'll need to show them something really original. Can't be a painting or anything, you know, *representational*.'

'Representational?' Eustace queried.

'Well, *obvious*. I had this idea. A big fish. In a tank.'

'Won't it rot?'

'Preserved in formaldehyde. What do you think?'

Eustace considered this at length.

'What kind of fish?' he asked at last.

'A swordfish maybe ... or a shark.'

'Where would you get hold of a shark?'

'I've got a mate who works in a fishmonger's, Brixton way,' said Gaz enthusiastically. 'Says if I can wait he should be able to get hold of a big fish for a couple of quid. Dunno how, but who cares?'

'And the tank? And the formaldehyde?'

'I found a tank on a skip, believe it or not. Well, Rodney actually found it, but I've got it. And as for formaldehyde – we work in a hospital, don't we?'

They had stopped side by side at a red light. Eustace turned a look of profound scepticism on his oldest friend.

'You're mad,' he pronounced, finally. 'Nobody's going to buy a dead shark in formaldehyde. It's a terrible idea. And anyway, how is that art?'

'You need to broaden your horizons,' Gaz said good humouredly. 'This sort of stuff is the future, Tutty, the future. Mark my words.'

The lights turned to green.

19 February

Eustace found himself in Crouch End for a second successive Thursday evening, though this time he arrived no more than half an hour early. He decided, on reflection, to give the pub a miss, and instead spent the thirty minutes he had at his disposal standing unnaturally close to the Clock Tower and, for want of any obvious alternative entertainment, watching the arrival and departure of customers at Budgens supermarket.

Time passed extraordinarily slowly. The five minutes between seven thirty and seven thirty-five were the slowest of the lot. Eustace could have sworn he'd been waiting half an hour. To his relief (and consternation) though, the hands on his watch appeared to acquire some unexpected momentum, and he was more than pleased to note that, at eight o'clock sharp, Amy Wildsmith was there. She looked, he thought, even more like the young Julie Christie than he remembered her looking (if that was possible) and was dressed this evening in a fashionably scruffy overcoat and leather boots.

'Well, I do declare,' she said theatrically, as if it was as much as she could manage not to burst into fits of laughter, 'Eustace Tutt. Decided to turn up this time, did you?'

She looked him up and down.

'Yes,' he said. 'I ... I thought I'd better.'

'Ha!' she cackled. 'Feared for your gonads, did you?'

Uncertainly, and not without a palpable degree of nervousness, Eustace advanced and kissed her cheek. To his not inconsiderable surprise, he felt the gesture reciprocated.

'I hope you're hungry,' she said, setting off in the direction of the pub where Eustace had made the acquaintance of Seamus O'Mahony precisely seven nights earlier. 'I could murder a vindaloo myself.'

Having no idea what Amy envisaged for their evening together, but acknowledging that his failure to show for their first date placed him at her mercy, Eustace had done his best to be prepared for all eventualities. To that end he had drunk no alcohol or valerian tea, and had eaten only a packet of pork scratchings, which he'd purchased from Mrs Rasmussen on his way home from the hospital.

'Sounds good to me,' he said with what he himself could hear to be slightly excessive enthusiasm. 'Where are we going then?'

'The Bamboo Hut. Best vindaloo for miles around.'

Eustace discovered that if he walked very quickly he could just keep up with her. However, as a result he found himself embarrassingly short of breath by the time they reached their destination, for all it was no more than five hundred yards along the Broadway from the Clock Tower.

'You're not a vegetarian, are you?' demanded Amy once they were installed at a table in the window of the restaurant.

'No,' Eustace confirmed, then, as if to contradict himself, 'I mean, no.'

It struck him, as he said it, that if he *was* a vegetarian he would deny it.

'That's all right, then,' she went on, taking a packet of Woodbines from her bag. 'I don't think that would have worked. I'm going to have the chicken vindaloo, boiled rice and a poppadum. What about you?'

'I'll go with your recommendation,' said Eustace. He couldn't help feeling he was being tested. To have ordered anything milder than a vindaloo would have shown weakness, and he was painfully aware that his non-appearance the week before had left him with some goodwill to retrieve. There was no way he was going to admit that he'd never eaten a vindaloo in his life. His closest encounter to date consisted of sitting at a table with friends who'd taken more ale than was good for them and, in a spirit of intoxicated bravura, ordering the hottest dish on the menu at the Bay of Bengal. All he now recalled of that occasion was their perspiring faces and claims that eating vindaloo was akin to eating hot coals. It was thus with some trepidation that he awaited the arrival of their meal.

In fact Eustace discovered that if he ate the vindaloo in very small mouthfuls it was perfectly manageable. He was relieved to note that he did not even appear to be perspiring. Nevertheless, he was conscious that he lacked the courage to attack his meal with the gusto with which Amy was attacking hers. They ate in silence, Amy inevitably finishing before Eustace. She watched him eat his last few mouthfuls.

'Right,' she said then, taking a Woodbine from the packet she'd placed strategically on the table, 'tell me everything.'

'Everything?'

'The story of your life to date in the Metropolis.'

34

'Okay,' Eustace agreed, hesitantly. 'I'll need a cigarette for that, though.'

Amy offered him a Woodbine. He had the strong impression he was expected to accept, so he did.

He told her about the squat on the Clerkenwell/ Bloomsbury border, about Gaz and the Germans; he told her what little he could about Rodney on the top floor; about the hospital and Mrs Clout; about Mrs Rasmussen's shop and Seamus O'Mahony's magazine. Most of what he said bore more than a passing resemblance to some truth or other, though he found himself curiously unable to resist a little exaggeration in the territory of the Germans. From his account, Amy was left wondering if they even possessed any clothes.

'And have you in fact written anything?' she asked, when he seemed to have no more to say.

'I spent the whole weekend writing,' Eustace assured her. 'I've got this thing about being a poet, a proper published poet, by the time I'm twenty-one.'

'When's that?'

'29th July.'

Amy considered this. 'No time to waste, then,' she said, finally. 'Hey, isn't that the date of the royal wedding?'

Eustace nodded. 'Makes it worse somehow'.

Amy lit another Woodbine. 'Sounds to me like you need a plan,' she said. 'I'll see what I can do. Meanwhile, I need your help.'

'Oh?'

'Saturday week. Oxford Street. I'm staging a happening: a picnic on a traffic island. Fancy coming?'

Eustace had only the vaguest idea of what might constitute a happening, but was so taken aback to receive a request rather than a command from Amy Wildsmith that he agreed immediately.

'Sounds brilliant,' he said, enthusiastically. 'What are we having?'

'Champagne and caviar,' she replied.

'Really?'

'Well, Pomagne and lumpfish.'

'Oh.'

'And Bath Oliver biscuits.'

'Count me in.'

'Great. Now can you get some of your friends to drop by and join us at different points in the afternoon? They can be the audience participation.'

Eustace thought of Gaz and the Germans. Could they be persuaded? He thought so.

'Yeh, I'm sure that won't be a problem.'

'And do you know anyone with a good camera? We'll need a record of it.'

'Gaz has got a Zenith,' said Eustace. 'Weighs a ton, but it takes pretty good photos.'

'Perfect. I knew you'd come up trumps, Eustace Tutt.' She flashed him a winning smile. 'Although I must confess I had my doubts about your reliability this time last week.'

'Yes, sorry about that,' Eustace began, 'it was really very...'

She dismissed his explanations with a wave of her hand.

'Oh forget it,' she said. 'Let's go and have a drink.'

She called for the bill.

O'Mahony was installed in the pub when they got there. He looked up as they entered, managing somehow to ask Eustace with his eyebrows if he would prefer not to be recognised. Eustace indicated through a variety of facial contortions that he would. O'Mahony nodded, winked, and turned his attention back to the slim volume in front of him.

'Mine's a Famous Grouse,' Amy announced, taking a seat at the table next to O'Mahony's. 'A little water, no ice.'

'Oh, right,' said Eustace uncertainly. He made his way

in, but he quickly sensed that this would constitute a grave error of judgement.

'You're welcome,' was therefore all he said.

'See you Saturday week, then. I'll meet you outside Collets, Charing Cross Road, at two o'clock. Okay?'

'Fine.'

'And Eustace, don't stop off at any pubs on your way. I need you to be on time. All right?'

'I'll be there,' Eustace assured her. 'You can count on it.'

Once again she kissed him on the cheek, then the door was closed and Eustace stood alone on the doorstep. With an unvoiced sigh, he turned and walked in the direction of the bus stop. All too soon it would be six a.m. and time to get up. Mrs Clout would be expecting him at seven and she was not a woman whose disapproval he could contemplate any more of. He prayed to the God he did not believe in for a short wait at the bus stop.

22 February

'So the idea is a picnic in the middle of Oxford Street?' asked Hilde, her intonation, which normally gave nothing away, betraying significant incredulity. Eustace nodded.

'And this is called a *happening*?' Hanne went on.

'Apparently,' Eustace agreed.

'Sounds bonkers to me,' Gaz observed. 'Who has a picnic in February? It might snow.'

'I think that's the point. Sort of,' said Eustace. It was Sunday evening and he was sitting at the kitchen table at the squat with Gaz, Hannelore and Hildegard. Rodney, as usual, was somewhere else.

The Germans exchanged a glance.

'Okay,' said Hilde. 'We'll come. We were going to spend next weekend reading Nietzsche, but we can take a break from that, I suppose.'

Hanne nodded in agreement. Eustace looked at them quizzically. He was still some way from acquiring the skill of determining when they were being serious. From their expressions, he inclined to the view that their plans for the weekend probably did involve Nietzsche, but he wouldn't have put money on it.

'Gaz?' he asked.

Gaz emitted a theatrical sigh.

'All right,' he agreed reluctantly. 'But I still think it's bonkers.'

'And could you bring your camera? Amy needs a few photos.'

'Doesn't want much, this girlfriend of yours, does she?' Gaz said. 'All right, Tutty. Never let it be said I refused to give Cupid a helping hand.'

'Don't call me Tutty,' muttered Eustace, half-heartedly.

'Sorry. I'll be there, and so will my camera. Now can we go to the pub? I could murder a pint.'

'You boys will have to go without us, I'm afraid,' said Hanne. 'We have important business.'

Eustace looked at Gaz, who shrugged.

'*Also sprach Zarathustra,*' Hilde elaborated. 'Nietzsche.'

Eustace reached for his Gauloises. Nietzsche could not, for the moment, compete with the Earth and Stars.

28 February

The day of the happening dawned grey and drizzly. Eustace emerged early from his basement room, no longer able to sleep. He stared gloomily out of the kitchen window and contemplated the day ahead of him.

He understood that the happening constituted some kind of test for him. He recalled with surprise Amy's forgiveness of his unforgiveable failure to appear on the occasion of their first … their first what? Date? Appointment? Meeting? He really couldn't say.

When thinking became difficult his response was generally to reach for a cigarette and make a cup of tea. This is what he did now, and thus Hannelore found him when she appeared wearing a tee-shirt that extended very slightly below her waist and bore the legend *Atomkraft – Nein danke!* and a pair of flip-flops.

'You shouldn't smoke so much, Eustace,' she said, before putting the kettle on. 'Or you will fulfil your ambition to die young sooner than you think.'

'Sorry,' muttered Eustace, stubbing out the offending cigarette without thinking. It took several more moments, which Eustace spent in idle contemplation of what he could see of Hannelore's bottom as she stood at the sink washing up cups, for him to be struck by what she had said.

'What do you mean, I want to die young?' he asked in some consternation.

She turned to face him and he immediately tried to focus his attention on her eyes.

'Well, don't you?' she challenged. 'Your great hero Rimbaud, he didn't exactly – how do you say? – do old bones, did he?'

'*Make* old bones.'

'And you drink too much and smoke too much,' she said. 'And take too many drugs.'

'Fat chance of that!' Eustace snorted sardonically.

'Well, you would if you could,' Hannelore went on, joining him at the table.

Eustace conceded the point.

'And you spend too much time in that dungeon of yours in the basement. You need to spend more time in the light.'

'You think so?'

'Of course. We have only one life, Eustace. We should do what we can to make it a long one and to live it properly.'

Eustace stared at her blankly, astounded by her bold certainties, which were so remote from anything he had ever experienced.

'You should read Nietzsche,' she said. 'In English translation, if you must.'

Eustace nodded thoughtfully, but lit another cigarette nevertheless.

It wasn't that Eustace had never asked himself if he was (so to speak) in *love* with Amy Wildsmith. But the realisation that he *was* struck him forcefully, and between the eyeballs as he gazed upon her in a deck chair on a traffic island in Oxford Street, a picnic hamper at her feet, a glass of Pomagne in her hand and a copy of *Cosmopolitan* on her lap. Something by Vivaldi – not *The Four Seasons*, but something Eustace vaguely recognised, with plenty of violin – was playing from a tinny transistor radio, audible only during brief lulls in the West End traffic. A parasol completed the picture, though the day had continued overcast and grey. Amy was dressed elegantly, if eccentrically, in a long summer dress and strappy sandals complemented by a fake fur jacket and a Russian hat.

'Tutty!'

Eustace stared.

'Tutty!'

Eustace came to with a start and turned to Gaz, who was standing on the pavement beside him outside Our Price Records.

'Don't call me Tutty,' he shouted automatically.

'Shall I take a photo now?'

'I don't know. I suppose so, yes.'

Gaz's extraordinarily heavy Russian camera hung around his neck. Slowly and deliberately he removed it from its case and set about the task of composing the frame. This involved several adjustments and took some time.

'Hurry up, for fuck's sake,' said Eustace.

'Keep your hair on, Tutty,' Gaz returned. 'This is a sophisticated bit of kit I've got here. State of the art Soviet technology.'

When he was finally ready, the operation was delayed

further by the untimely arrival of a number 8 bus, which transposed itself between photographer and subject for a full two minutes before moving off towards Tottenham Court Road. Gaz was quick to seize the moment. The noise made by the shutter sounded unnaturally loud to Eustace against the feeble backdrop of Vivaldi.

'What happens now?' asked Gaz.

'I don't know. I guess we join her for Champagne and caviar.'

'Looks like Pomagne and lumpfish to me,' said Gaz.

When traffic allowed, they crossed to the picnic, but by the time they reached Amy O'Mahony had appeared from somewhere and was raising a glass to them. For his part, he appeared to have entered into the spirit of the occasion, and sported a tweed suit and plus fours.

'Greetings, gentlemen,' he said, grinning broadly.

'Hello, boys,' smiled Amy, standing up and treating them both to a peck on the cheek. 'You'll have a glass of Pomagne, I'm sure.'

'I'd love one,' Gaz assured her gamely.

Eustace became aware for the first time of the gaze of passers-by, all of whom seemed to be looking in their direction, though none were sufficiently interested to stop and really stare. As they sipped Pomagne from plastic flutes and nibbled Bath Oliver biscuits spread thinly with lumpfish, Eustace became aware of a very tall woman standing on the opposite pavement, wearing a trench coat and green wellingtons and holding a clipboard.

'Who's that?' he asked Amy, indicating the woman with a not very subtle nod of his head.

'Oh, that's my tutor,' said Amy airily. 'I told you this was assessed, didn't I?'

'I'm not sure you did, actually,' Eustace replied.

O'Mahony was chasing a particularly scabrous-looking pigeon away, and Gaz was contorting himself to achieve a photograph from the most artistic angle when the

Germans appeared. Hannelore immediately seated herself in the only deckchair, which Amy had vacated to prepare more Bath Olivers, while Hildegard poured them both a glass of Pomagne.

'Hilde, Hanne, this is Amy,' said Gaz, who seemed now to have run out of film.

'Oh, hello,' Amy smiled, handing them each a Bath Oliver. 'I wondered if you'd been invited. Not that gatecrashers aren't welcome…'

'I met a man once who gatecrashed a happening,' O'Mahony volunteered, 'but it was a long time ago, and on the other side of the pond.'

As if on cue, a tramp arrived and held out his hand. Amy furnished him with a Bath Oliver and a flute of Pomagne.

'I'm a gentleman of the road, but today I live like a king!' he announced, before cramming the biscuit into his mouth whole and washing it down with Pomagne. He belched loudly, with evident satisfaction.

'You're a lady and a … and a gentleman, madam,' he declared, bowing to Amy before shuffling off across Oxford Street.

At that point the woman in the trench coat put her clipboard under her arm and strode off. A rather flustered-looking policeman arrived on the scene.

'You can't have a picnic here,' he announced to no-one in particular.

'Really?' returned Amy sweetly.

'You're causing an obstruction,' he elaborated. 'You'll have to pack up and go somewhere else. Regent's Park, for example.'

'It's a happening, officer,' explained O'Mahony, helpfully.

'Well it's not happening here, not any more. Now, you've got five minutes to pack up and clear off. Or else.'

'Or else what, officer?' enquired Hannelore, affecting

a strong German accent Eustace had never heard before.

'Or else,' replied the officer deliberately, and giving every indication of exhibiting a degree of restraint that was well beyond the call of duty, 'happening or no happening, I'll have you for obstruction. All of you.'

'In that case,' said Hildegard, now also affecting a cod German accent, but in a spirit of generous magnanimity, 'we'll go.'

'To Regent's Park,' said Amy. 'An excellent idea. The pollution here is shocking. Thanks very much for the tip, officer.'

'You're welcome, Miss,' sniffed the policeman, apparently mollified.

It took a matter of moments to pack up beneath his watchful gaze. Eustace and Amy carried the hamper, O'Mahony the parasol, Hannelore the deckchair, and Hildegard the open bottle of Pomagne and the transistor radio. Gaz judged the Zenith around his neck to be burden enough. They trudged across Oxford Street and headed north.

They finished the picnic in Regent's Park. It transpired that the hamper was stuffed with the following: quail eggs (hard boiled), Oxo-flavoured crisps, a hand-raised pork pie, new potatoes, and a salad containing different varieties of leaf. There was also a cold sausage, sliced. The consensus was that, as a picnic, it lacked the intrinsic interest of the happening, but that the park provided a significantly more appealing environment.

'And that's the whole point, of course,' said Amy as if she'd explained everything and they all duly nodded sagely, except Hildegard, who, after a moment's reflection, asked: 'What is?'

When there was no more Pomagne to be drunk or lumpfish to be eaten, Amy packed up the picnic and hailed a taxi.

'Thank you all very much,' she said graciously as she

climbed into the back of a black cab, and hamper, parasol, deckchair and transistor were passed into her. 'I hope you all feel you've been part of something bigger than yourselves this afternoon. Bye.'

The taxi pulled away and the five of them stood on the pavement and watched it disappear.

'That's quite a woman you have there, Eustace,' O'Mahony remarked.

Eustace looked at him dumbly.

'Is she completely mad, though?' asked Hannelore.

1 March

Well, was she? Mad?

The next morning Eustace lay in bed and contemplated Hannelore's question. She was certainly eccentric. But mad? No, on balance he thought not. He glanced at his watch – twenty-five to ten – and reached for a cigarette. The rest of Sunday lay ahead of him. From his basement room he was just able to see some evidence that the sun was shining, somewhere else. He lit up, blew smoke rings, and wondered what to do with the day.

A knock at his door shook Eustace out of his reverie.

'Come in.'

Hannelore entered. She was completely naked apart from her customary pair of flip-flops. Though Eustace was accustomed to this by now, he felt an immediate and, by now, annoyingly predictable stirring in his loins; he re-arranged his duvet.

'I've brought you a present, Eustace,' said Hannelore, sitting on his bed. Her left breast in all its shapely perfection was directly in his line of vision. He stubbed out his cigarette in the ashtray on his bedside table. She held a battered Penguin Classic in front of his eyes, obscuring his view of her breast.

'Nietzsche,' she explained. 'In English. I found it in a charity shop yesterday. 20p. Imagine, Eustace, your life could be transformed for 20p.'

'Thanks,' muttered Eustace. 'That's very kind.'

He was finding it very difficult to concentrate on anything other than his basest carnal desires at that moment. If Hannelore had not made it so abundantly clear to him through her every word, gesture and look since they'd met that whatever feelings, if any, he provoked in her, desire was not among them, he might have been tempted to draw an inappropriate inference from her appearance in his room naked down to her flip-flops. As it was, he concentrated on concealing his erection while simultaneously wishing she would leave or, alternatively, stay, so that he could contemplate her physical perfection at leisure (since he was sufficiently realistic to acknowledge that the likelihood of her clambering into bed on top of him – his preferred option – was close to non-existent). In the event she satisfied both his second choice options, getting up from the bed and performing a series of stretches at the window before taking her leave.

'Thanks again,' called Eustace as she left the room. At that moment he was thinking that the proportions of her buttocks were as perfect as the proportions of her breasts. Callipygian, was that the word for her?

'You're welcome,' she called nonchalantly over her shoulder. 'It was only 20p.' When the door had closed behind her, Eustace lifted his duvet and regretfully contemplated his detumescence.

It proved to be a profoundly unsatisfactory day. Eustace had spent some considerable time recalling every detail of Hannelore's body before he finally managed to drag himself out of bed, with frustration and despondency fighting an evenly matched battle to be declared his prevailing emotion of the moment. The kitchen bore all the traces of those who had had breakfast there – Eustace was convinced he could smell black pudding, allegedly favoured as a Sunday treat by the elusive Rodney – but there was no sign that it had occurred to anyone to wash up or clear away. Catching sight of a puddle of congealed egg yolk on one of the plates abandoned on the table, Eustace decided on a whim to cycle to Crouch End and pay Amy a surprise visit. They might, he thought, evaluate the success of yesterday's happening over a leisurely coffee. Amy might even decide (he thought further) that it was time to open up and declare her feelings for him. Perhaps she would suggest that they spend the afternoon in bed. As this thought struck him, Eustace became aware that his pace on the stair had quickened. Very soon he was on his bicycle and heading north up Gray's Inn Road.

It was unfortunate that he got lost somewhere between Caledonian Road and Finsbury Park. A Rastafarian was keen to help, but proved less than precise when giving directions. He seemed to be saying that if Eustace wanted to get to Crouch End, he should consider starting from somewhere else. On Green Lanes Eustace's bicycle chain started to misbehave, which slowed his progress further. By the time he finally reached Crouch End Broadway it was early afternoon and Eustace's mood had darkened. When, obediently waiting at a red light, he saw Amy emerge from an Italian restaurant a mere few yards ahead of him, arm in arm with a young man of classic yet somehow extraordinary good looks, he was unsurprised to note his mood blacken even further. The lights changed to green, but Eustace remained where he was. He watched Amy and her unknown companion disappear into the distance, their body language, he felt, telling him considerably more than he wanted to know.

He needed a drink. He found a railing to chain his bike to and made swiftly for the pub, arriving just as the barmaid called time. He cursed loudly.

'You look like a man in need of a drink,' observed O'Mahony, who had clearly been seated at his usual table for some considerable time and seen off more than the pint of Guinness he was about to finish.

'Yes,' was all Eustace could say by way of reply.

'Then you'd better come back to my place,' said O'Mahony, gathering up the piles of papers from the table and unceremoniously quaffing the last of his Guinness. 'I may just have a bottle of whiskey we can do justice to. And you could even tell me why you're in such dire need of a drink.'

They walked to Turnpike Lane. O'Mahony produced a bottle of Powers, and they drank their way through the rest of the afternoon. Eustace unburdened himself to O'Mahony, who shook his head sagely and opined that there was no fathoming some women, and that was a fact.

By early evening, Eustace's senses were, once again, well and truly deranged. He staggered back to the Broadway to collect his bike, only·to be confronted by the fact of its absence. All that remained was the chain. In truth, this may have saved his life for he was in no condition to ride a bicycle back to Clerkenwell. He cursed, walked towards the Clock Tower and waited an exceptionally long time for a bus.

2 March

Eustace slept fitfully and little, finally abandoning the attempt at about five thirty the next morning. He was frantically searching the cupboards in the kitchen for something (anything) to dull the pain when Gaz came upon him.

'Jesus, Tutty, you look grim. What the fuck's happened?'

Eustace scowled at him. 'Some bastard stole my bike.'.

'And that's why you look like death?'

'Yes. No. Sort of. Look, have you got any aspirin?'

Gaz was able to oblige, and after two aspirin and several mugs of PG Tips, Eustace was able to open his eyes a fraction and even believe in the possibility that death might not be imminent. The prospect of a cigarette, though, remained a prospect too far.

'Are you coming to work?' Gaz ventured to ask.

'Bus,' Eustace answered, surprising himself with the clarity of his thought. 'I'll have to take the bus.'

'Okay, I'll see you there,' said Gaz.

In the forty-five minutes it took Eustace to get to the hospital, the physical pain resulting from the abuse of O'Mahony's whiskey faded in direct proportion to the emergence of the pain of his terrible humiliation by Amy Wildsmith. And Eustace realised that there is pain much worse than the purely physical. It was beyond the capacity of any aspirin to take away the wretchedness provoked by the sight of the woman he now knew he loved in the intimate company of another.

The morning passed as if happening to someone else. He heard Mrs Clout's caustic remarks about his physical appearance, but far away and as if addressed elsewhere. He felt no connection between his hands and the mop he was apparently using to clean the floor of the sluice on renal. He watched Gaz's lips move as they sat together over coffee in the hospital canteen, but didn't connect the movement with speech, or make any attempt to decode whatever was emanating from his friend's mouth.

At half past two or thereabouts, having eaten nothing since his arrival at the hospital, drunk two black coffees and smoked a solitary cigarette, he was suddenly struck by the words: *The fee of all desire is paid in pain.* Since he was still at some remove from functioning normally, it took him some moments to comprehend that he might have been struck by the first line of a poem. Thank God the staff nurse was at the nurses' station: for whatever unfathomable reason she seemed frequently entertained by Eustace, and had even been known to smile at him. He was able to borrow a pen and procure a sheet of paper, with which he disappeared into the broom cupboard. He turned on the light, locked himself in, and began laboriously to write.

18 March

When Eustace got home, late as usual because he was now subject to the vagaries of London buses, he found a letter waiting for him. It was the first he had received since his arrival in the capital, and he recognised the handwriting immediately. Someone – Rodney ? – had propped it up against the mug he'd drunk tea from that morning, and omitted to wash up. Eustace reached automatically for the Gauloises in his coat pocket, extracted one and lit up before picking up the offending mug, washing it up, scanning the kitchen for any further washing-up that might need doing, moving a pile of plates from one cupboard to another, turning the radio on and off, and walking round the kitchen table several times in each direction. He then sat down and stared at the unopened letter.

'You're afraid to open it.'

Startled, Eustace looked up to see Hannelore standing in the doorway.

'It's from your mother, perhaps,' she went on, 'and you're feeling guilty because you've been in London for months and you haven't phoned her or written to her. You probably owe her money. You feel bad about it and you don't want to think about what she's written to you. Even the washing-up is preferable to this.'

Eustace stared at her blankly.

'How do you know all that?' he asked finally.

'Elementary, when you've read as much Sherlock Holmes as I have,' she returned. 'The longer you leave this, the harder it will become. Open the letter, Eustace, and read. How bad can it be?'

My Dear Eustace (he read)

> *I hope this letter finds you well. In fact, I hope this letter finds you. (Do they deliver to squats?) Your father*

and I are both well, although we have been worried about you. It's been quite a while since you left and we've heard nothing from you. I know how lonely London can be, so I hope you've made some good friends and are getting on well. It must be nice to live with someone like Gary – you two go back such a long way. Perhaps you have even got a job? I know these are difficult times but that makes it more important to have a plan. Have you thought about contacting the University to see if they'll have you back? Your father and I were saying only this morning that we still don't understand what happened or why you left. It seems such a shame. No-one in the family had ever been to university before, and we were both so proud when you got in.

Eustace, your father and I wanted to say that there's no need for you to pay back the money you borrowed when you left. We were happy to help you start out in London. But we would like to see you. We're coming up on the train next month – on the 11th – and we thought we'd come straight over to your "squat" from Charing Cross (Gary's mum gave us the address). Dad thinks we'll be there about 11.30.

We're both really looking forward to seeing you, Eustace, and to taking you out for dinner. Dad sends his best regards.

All my love
Mum xxx

Eustace finished reading and put the letter down on the table. What were 'best regards'? Why had his father sent them? Had he actually said the words *Do give the boy my best regards, Dorothy*?

'Well?' asked Hannelore.

Eustace had forgotten she was there.

'They're coming to visit,' said Eustace. 'Next month.'

'Great!' said Hannelore. 'We'll bake a cake.'

'11th April,' he added.

'We'll bake biscuits, then. I can't wait to meet them. Rodney's mother came here once. She's very glamorous, used to be a model. Hilde baked a carrot cake and she loved it. And don't worry, Eustace, we'll put on some clothes in honour of the occasion. I think I have some somewhere.'

It was only then that Eustace noticed that Hannelore was, yet again, completely naked (though a small part of her thigh was concealed by the towel she was carrying). He wondered if he was starting to lose his mind.

'Thanks,' he managed to mutter.

'Don't mention it,' said Hannelore lightly.

He watched her buttocks disappear in the direction of the bathroom, was struck again by the word *callipygian*, and felt that familiar ache of desire. He noted, with some satisfaction this time, that the fee of all desire was truly paid in pain.

I I April

Eustace felt so depressed at the prospect of his parents' impending visit that he needed several cups of valerian tea to get to sleep the night before, and then didn't wake until after eleven the next morning. He came to with a start, pulled on some clothes and made his way upstairs to the kitchen. Hannelore and Hildegard were both sitting at the table, fully clothed as promised, and the kitchen was warm with the smell of baking.

'The biscuits are in the oven,' Hildegard announced proudly.

'Three varieties,' Hannelore added. 'All traditional German recipes. Your parents will love them, I'm sure.'

'Uh, thanks,' said Eustace. 'Thanks a lot. Where's Gaz?'

'Gone to Brixton,' said Hannelore. 'They may have a fish for him.'

Eustace raised an eyebrow.

'For his art, remember?' added Hildegard helpfully. 'The fish in formaldehyde?'

'Oh yes.' Eustace nodded vaguely. 'The pickled fish. Look, it's really good of you two to go to so much trouble for my mum and dad.'

'It's our pleasure,' Hannelore assured him. 'What we do for Rodney's mother we must also do for yours. Your father, too, of course.'

At that moment there was a knock at the door. Eustace glanced at the clock. It was precisely 11.30.

'That'll be them,' he said gloomily.

'I'll put the kettle on,' said Hildegard.

Eustace nodded thanks, took a deep breath and went downstairs. He paused, took another before opening the door. His parents stood on the step, his father in a car coat (although they'd come by train), his mother in a bright green ensemble that included an improbable hat.

'Eustace! Oh Eustace!' she exclaimed, as if he was the last person she was expecting. 'It's so good to see you!' (Every exclamation mark was clearly audible.) She reached out, hugged him to her and planted a kiss on his forehead.

'Morning, son,' said his father gruffly.

Quentin and Dorothy Tutt received a much warmer welcome from the Germans than their elusive progeny had managed to provide.

'Mr and Mrs Tutt,' said Hildegard. 'Welcome to our home. Please take a seat.'

'I'm Hannelore,' said Hannelore.

'And I'm Hildegard,' said Hildegard.

Hands were shaken and the proffered seats at the kitchen table taken.

'But you can call me Hilde,' Hilde went on.

'And me Hanne,' added Hanne.

(Almost like a double act, thought Eustace.)

'Please call me ... Dorothy,' reciprocated Dorothy uncomfortably.

'And I'm ... ahem,' (much clearing of the throat) 'Quentin.'

'We're very pleased to meet you at last,' said Hilde.

Eustace began to feel distinctly superfluous.

There was a brief silence.

'Is Gary not here?' asked Dorothy eventually.

'Gary went to Brixton,' said Hannelore, 'to find a fish. For his art.'

Dorothy nodded knowingly. Quentin wondered if she had said 'art' or 'heart'.

'Brixton?' he said. 'Isn't that rather dangerous?'

'Dangerous?' echoed Eustace, strangely grateful for an opportunity to enter the conversation.

'Something I read in the *Mail*,' Quentin explained. 'Gangs of youths. Marauding.'

'Marauding?' echoed Eustace (was that really all he was? An echo of his father?).

'I haven't heard anything about it,' said Hannelore, 'but in Brixton anything is possible.'

'Anyway, Gaz has gone there for a fish,' said Hilde, as if to draw the topic to a conclusion.

'And you must both be – ' (Hanne paused, searching for the idiom) ' – gasping for a cup of tea.'

'And we have baked German biscuits,' added Hilde. 'We'll make a pot of tea and leave you in peace. You must have so much to discuss with Eustace.'

Eustace looked helplessly at his housemates. It also seemed to him that his parents were shifting on their chairs at this announcement of imminent departure. He reached for a cigarette. Dorothy averted her gaze. Quentin harrumphed.

When the tea was made, the Germans, as good as their word, withdrew. There was a long uncomfortable silence. Eustace seemed to hear himself smoking.

'Shall I be mother?' asked Dorothy when the tea had brewed for a good five minutes. Eustace was reminded that she could sometimes achieve something approaching wit; not something Quentin could ever be accused of.

She duly poured, and passed round the biscuits, which

were still warm from the oven. 'They seem like very nice girls, your Germans,' she observed.

('Why *my* Germans?' Eustace wondered antagonistically, but managed not to say.) He attempted an inscrutable smile by way of response.

'So, how's it all going, then, this London adventure of yours?' asked Quentin when he and his wife had both eaten a biscuit and Eustace had consumed several, between ever more manic drags on his cigarette.

('Why *adventure*?' thought Eustace crossly before congratulating himself on managing, once again, not to give voice to his feelings.)

'Great,' he replied so unconvincingly that he wouldn't have convinced himself, even if he had believed what he was saying. 'No, really' (this in response to an imagined or anticipated challenge) 'it's all going really well.'

'Got a job?' asked Quentin, as Eustace had known he would.

'Assistant editor,' he replied, 'on *Scripsi*. It's a literary magazine.'

'Oh that's nice,' said Dorothy. 'What does it involve?'

Eustace elaborated on his role as O'Mahony's assistant, carefully avoiding any reference to the quantity of alcohol that typically fuelled their editorial deliberations. When he'd finished Quentin scratched his chin.

'I've never heard of *Scripsi*,' he said. 'Does it have a big circulation?'

'It's a Literary magazine, Dad,' Eustace explained patiently. 'They never have big circulations.'

'So I suppose this job doesn't pay much, then?' Quentin went on relentlessly.

'It doesn't pay at all,' Eustace exploded in exasperation. 'I do it for nothing.'

'Nothing at all?' asked Dorothy, incredulous.

'Nothing at all,' Eustace confirmed.

'Then how in heaven do you keep body and soul together?' asked Quentin. 'Benefits?'

'No, don't worry, dad, your taxes aren't funding my tobacco habit. Well, not directly, anyway.'

'Meaning?'

Eustace realised that he had no option other than to come clean.

'The NHS pays me. I'm a domestic in a hospital.'

'A domestic?' Dorothy repeated.

'A cleaner. I clean floors, loos, the odd sink. It's tough, but someone's got to do it.'

Quentin looked at his son in disbelief.

'So that's what you left university for,' he said, more in sorrow than in anger. 'To be a cleaner.'

Eustace could have countered that: firstly, he hadn't so much *left* university as been summarily ejected; secondly, whatever the manner of his departure from that august seat of learning, he had manifestly not left with the express intention of becoming a cleaner; and, thirdly, given the current rate of unemployment brought about by the government that he, Quentin Oliver Tutt, had no doubt helped elect, it was actually remarkable and cause for celebration that he had been able to find a job of any complexion. However, he said none of these things. His response (he felt) was gloriously monosyllabic.

'Yes.'

His only consolation was that this encounter with his parents was going no worse than he had feared.

Lunch, at a café near the British Museum, was a largely silent affair. Eustace noted with some surprise that Dorothy chose the lasagna from the specials board. Quentin went for shepherd's pie. And Eustace, strangely unable to focus on the task of making a choice, selected the all day breakfast. This involved two pork sausages, two rashers of bacon, two fried eggs, a little heap of grilled mushrooms and a fried slice. Eustace discovered to his surprise that his appetite was immense.

'Looks as if you needed that,' Quentin remarked tartly when he'd finished.

'Yes,' Eustace agreed. The monosyllabic affirmative was in some danger of becoming his stock response to his father's questions, whether disguised as observations or not.

It rained. 'Does it rain a lot in London?' said Dorothy aloud.

Eustace didn't reply. It seemed no reply was expected.

With no plan, and nowhere obvious to go after lunch, the Tutts returned to the squat for coffee. The Germans were at their most obliging, fussing around Dorothy and Quentin, hanging up their wet coats, and generally making Eustace's inadequacies as a host ever more palpable.

Coffee poured, they had all just sat down at the kitchen table when there was a loud knock at the street door downstairs.

'I'll go!' said Eustace at once, springing up.

'Are you expecting someone, Eustace?' asked Hildegard.

'No. Yes. I mean, sort of.'

Quentin and Dorothy looked at Hildegard and Hannelore. Hildegard and Hannelore looked at Quentin and Dorothy. Quentin raised an eyebrow. Dorothy, unaccountably, started to hum. She seemed to be humming Danny Boy.

Downstairs the last person Eustace expected to find on the doorstep of the squat was Amy Wildsmith. Yet there, incontrovertibly, she stood.

'Amy!'

'Hello, Eustace. Can I come in?'

She didn't wait for a response, but walked past him and up the stairs to the kitchen. Eustace found himself wondering how she knew where she was going. Then he remembered he had bigger things to worry about. What had brought her here? And where was the impossibly good looking young man he'd seen her with in the street in Crouch End? He was caught between two competing impulses: to let himself out into the rain and lose himself in the anonymity of the city; or go upstairs and attempt to make some sense of whatever might be happening in the kitchen.

The temptation to flee was a very strong one. But just as he was about to slip out into the rain, he remembered Nietzsche, and Hannelore's advocacy of his philosophy. And strangely, at that moment, the prospect of confirming the Germans' darkest suspicions about him seemed to matter. He closed the door and felt for his cigarettes in his jeans pockets. They were, of course, in the kitchen. With no further reason to delay the moment, he followed Amy upstairs.

The interval was nevertheless long enough for formal introductions to have been completed by the time he entered the room. It was no doubt for this reason that five heads turned expectantly in his direction. Their collective silence shouted 'Take charge!' loudly at him.

'Has anyone seen my cigarettes?' he asked.

'Oh, Eustace!' His mother's disapproval could not have been more Pavlovian.

Amy took a packet of Woodbines from her pocket and offered them round. The Germans smiled and shook their heads. Quentin harrumphed. Dorothy looked into her lap. And Eustace took a cigarette gratefully, leaning forward as Amy struck a match for him.

'More coffee, anyone?' asked Hannelore.

'Yes please,' said Dorothy eagerly, scrambling for safe territory.

Hildegard poured her a cup.

Eustace heard himself humming. Was that really Danny Boy? He thrust the Woodbine between his lips.

'Have you had a nice day?' asked Amy, turning her most winning smile on Dorothy and Quentin.

'Oh yes,' said Dorothy. 'It's been lovely to see where Eustace is living. And to meet his new friends.'

Her hands reached out anxiously for the improbable hat, which had ended up across the table from her. She appeared disproportionately relieved to have it in her grasp.

'Lovely,' Quentin agreed unconvincingly, 'but we are going to have to leave shortly. Don't want to get back too late, and you know how the trains can be.'

The Germans nodded sympathetically.

'Was that the door?' asked Eustace, desperate now for any diversion. In fact it was. Footsteps were heard ascending the stairs. The door opened to reveal Gaz. He was holding a large fish in one hand and a bottle of olive oil in the other.

'God,' he said, 'it's all kicking off in Brixton. Fighting in the streets. Coppers everywhere. I was lucky to escape with my life. And the fish.'

'I told you,' said Quentin triumphantly to his son. 'Marauding youths. Oh yes.' Gaz seemed to notice the older Tutts for the first time.

'Oh hello, Mr Tutt, Mrs Tutt,' he said apologetically. 'I won't shake hands if you don't mind. Mine are a bit ... fishy.'

Later, Eustace lay in the dark in his room in the basement while Amy sat on the end of his bed smoking Woodbines.

'Can we talk?' she asked after a long silence.

'Talk?'

'Yes, talk. As in "communicate". Orally.'

'If you want. What is there to say?'

'You tell me. You haven't spoken to me since the day of the happening. Did something happen?'

(Was she being funny?)

'Happen?'

'Don't do that echoey thing, please, Eustace. You know it drives me mad.'

'Sorry.'

(Another long silence.)

'The day after the happening,' said Eustace, 'I cycled up to Crouch End. I was cycling along the Broadway when … Who *was* that man you were with? Or should I say *boy*?'

'What boy?'

'You came out of a restaurant. Arm in arm. He was young, very young. And very good looking. I suppose. If you go for that type.'

'Does it matter who he was?'

'Yes. No. Of course it does. A bit.'

There was another long silence in the darkness. Then Eustace felt the bed sag as Amy lay down next to him.

'Then it was my brother. My twin brother, as it happens.'

Eustace sat up.

'I don't believe you,' he said, but even as he said it he realised he did. Of course, there had been a strong family resemblance. And the Julie Christie thing. He could see it now.

'Well, that must be a matter for you,' said Amy haughtily. 'But I don't tell lies. As a general rule. It's an actor thing. You spend so long pretending to be someone else that if you told lies when you weren't doing that, you wouldn't know if it was New York or New Year. And I prefer to know where I am.'

Eustace reached out to her in the darkness and soon realised he was touching her breast.

'You can touch my breast,' said Amy, 'but only because you've had such a traumatic time. And not for long.'

In the event, he fell asleep with his hand on her breast; and very soon Amy was also dead to the world. Eustace dreamed that he woke up in a wood surrounded by a dozen or more Amys, some male, some female, some in-determinate. All of them seemed to be naked but wearing the same hat. It bore a distinct resemblance to the improb-able variety worn by Dorothy.

12 April

'He's only eaten my bloody fish!' Gaz complained bitterly. 'After all I went through to get it. Brixton. Risking my life. I don't believe it.'

'Who?' asked Amy.

'Rodney,' Gaz returned. 'The wombat in the attic.'

It was Sunday morning. Eustace and Amy had slept deeply and at length. When they had finally emerged, des-perately hungry and still befuddled from sleep some time after ten, it had been to find Gaz in the kitchen staring in disbelief at all that remained of the fish on a plate on the table: a very large bone.

'What happened?' asked Eustace as other parts of the world around him started to make sense again.

'I told you,' returned Gaz impatiently. 'Bloody Rodney ate my fish. Came down in the night, had the munchies, raided the fridge, I suppose. The wombat.'

'You left it in the fridge?' asked Amy.

'I was going to get the formaldehyde tomorrow. Needed to keep it as fresh as I could until then. No point now. No-one's going to buy a bloody fishbone in formaldehyde.'

'They might not have gone for the fish in formaldehyde either,' suggested Eustace helpfully.

'Oh for fuck's sake, Tutty,' Gaz almost wailed in an-guish, 'it was my big idea. My best idea. Ever.'

('Don't call me Tutty,' muttered Eustace.)

'I suppose you could get another fish,' said Amy.

'But not like that one,' Gaz complained. 'I waited weeks for it. It was perfect. And my interview's in ten days. I could kill bloody Rodney.'

'Have you seen him?' asked Eustace, putting the kettle on.

'His door's locked,' said Gaz, 'so he's either gone to ground or he's gone out. Fucking wombat.'

In the end, Amy removed the offending bone, Eustace made tea and then they all walked up Gray's Inn Road to King's Cross for breakfast at a greasy spoon. Gaz ordered scrambled eggs on toast, Eustace a bacon and egg sandwich and Amy a plate of kidneys.

'I suppose I could paint something,' said Gaz reflectively when they'd all finished. 'Not quite as cutting edge as the fish idea, but I was looking at those doors at the hospital on Friday. That might work. Big canvasses.'

Eustace and Amy looked at each other; simultaneously reached for their cigarettes.

'Yeh,' said Gaz to no-one in particular. 'That might work.'

Eustace felt his sense of impending doom more keenly than ever. True, he had survived the visit from his parents, for all that it could not honestly have been considered a resounding success. True, he was not only reconciled with Amy Wildsmith but had spent an entire night with his hand on her breast, which surely constituted the greatest intimacy achieved (with the woman in question, at least) to date. And true, he had somehow secured a position of some influence on a literary magazine, which he had come to understand was, if small, highly regarded among the cognoscenti who were aware of the existence of such publications.

Yet he was only too bitterly conscious of his 21st birthday, looming on the horizon and still, of course, scheduled to coincide (thanks to the malign influence of whatever dark forces pull the strings of synchronicity) with the wedding of the heir to the throne and Lady Diana Spencer. It mattered very little to Eustace that the majority of the population would go about their business on 29th July if anything less aware than ever before (given the really quite extraordinary fuss, in Eustace's judgment, that was being made of what, after all, was only a wedding when all was said and done) of the true significance of the day. He, Eustace Tiberius Tutt would know it was his 21st birthday and would be bitterly conscious that he had reached that milestone, that landmark, without having published a single line of poetry, while his hero, genius, poet and seer Arthur Rimbaud, had produced an impressive œuvre by that age, and was heading towards a brief, eventful retirement (from poetry, at least). True, Seamus O'Mahony had muttered the odd comment about poems Eustace had shown him that could be construed as encouraging. But in his bleaker moments Eustace suspected that the purpose of this encouragement was no more than to motivate him sufficiently to continue his many hours' unpaid labour to *Scripsi* without complaint. At times like this tobacco was his only solace. He reached across his desk to find an empty packet of Gauloises. Mrs Rasmussen's it was, then.

11 May
'Coming to the cabaret?' asked Gaz as he and Eustace cycled eastward towards the hospital early one Monday morning in May. Eustace had managed to replace his stolen bicycle with an even more rackety affair salvaged from a skip.

'What cabaret's that?' said Eustace with little interest.

'Amy's cabaret, of course. With Hanne and Hilde. Friday night.'

Eustace looked at his friend in astonishment. They had stopped at a traffic light and were two abreast.

'I don't know anything about it,' he admitted.

'Really? I thought Amy would have told you. She and some of her mates from the drama school. A kind of alternative variety show.'

Eustace was nonplussed.

'And what have the Germans got to do with it?' he said aloud.

'Reverse striptease,' said Gaz. 'They come on stage stark naked, then put their clothes on to music. Until they're wearing boiler suits, hats, boots, the lot. Amy's choreographed the whole thing. Can't wait to see it myself.'

The lights changed and they cycled on in silence. How could it be that Eustace knew nothing of this? Did he want to see it? How did he feel about Amy collaborating with the Germans? These were the questions he pondered as he mopped the floor of the sluice on the renal ward under the watchful gaze of Mrs Clout.

14 May

'Sounds a gas.' Such was O'Mahony's verdict on the news of the cabaret, delivered to Eustace across the kitchen table, where they were making a concerted effort to reduce the *Scripsi* slush pile. 'What time does it start?'

'I don't know,' Eustace complained. 'No-one's told me anything.'

'How d'you know about it, then?' said O'Mahony with irrefutable logic.

'Gaz told me,' Eustace admitted.

'Ah,' said O'Mahony, nodding knowingly. 'So it's the women who didn't tell you anything. I'll let you into a secret, Eustace: there's no accounting for the behaviour of a woman. Accept that, and straight away your life becomes a whole lot simpler. Believe me, I know.'

Eustace looked at him doubtfully, but O'Mahony was giving nothing away, drawing heavily on his cigarette and fixing his gaze on the manuscript in front of him, a quizzical expression on his face.

'Jesus, that's shite,' was his verdict. 'Rejection slip, please, Eustace – the brutal one. We don't want to be wasting any more time on drivel from him.'

Eustace duly passed the rejection slip.

'What do you mean exactly?' he asked.

'I mean it's absolute and utter shite and I never want to read another word from the pen of its author, who could not be more lacking in talent if he made it his life's work to be so.'

'No, about women,' said Eustace, 'about there being no accounting for women.'

'Oh that,' said O'Mahony, laying aside the next manuscript from the pile. 'Well, the first Mrs O'Mahony taught me never to expect any particular reaction to anything I ever said or did. Somehow I'd always get it wrong. If I expected gratitude I'd get anger, if I expected anger I'd get indifference. The only rule was that there was no rule. The second Mrs O'Mahony, well, she taught me that when you're having a conversation with a woman, you're never talking about the same thing. I'd think we were talking about personal responsibility in the twentieth century only to discover she'd really been asking why hadn't I put the dustbin out? And Mrs O'Mahony the third? She taught me that I understood nothing about women except that I understood nothing about women.'

'Oh, I see,' Eustace nodded. 'How many Mrs O'Mahonies have there been?'

'Oh, just the three. And there'll be no more. I was a man of means once, Eustace. Now look at me.' He gestured vaguely around the room, which, now that Eustace came to think about it, did exude something of an air of shabby poverty. 'I may be a cliché, but what I say is, clichés are clichés for a reason. Still,' he went on with a sudden change of mood, 'I like the idea of reverse striptease. Very creative. Very subversive. You can count me in for that one, Eustace.' And he returned to the slush pile.

15 May

Eustace, O'Mahony and Gaz occupied most of the front row in the tiny pub basement. Amy and the Germans, as key figures in the cabaret, were nowhere to be seen – presumably somewhere behind the heavy velvet curtain that hung at the back of the makeshift stage. Eustace, O'Mahony and Gaz sat in silence, having run out of speculation about the evening ahead of them. To talk about anything else just seemed somehow inappropriate.

There were very few empty seats, but the room could accommodate no more than thirty. The lights dimmed and Amy stepped onto the stage. She appeared to be wearing no more than a binliner yet somehow looked more like Julie Christie than ever.

'Good evening and welcome,' she began. 'Thank you for coming to our evening of alternative cabaret, which begins with existentialist comedian Kevin Smith.'

To a burst of sustained applause, Kevin Smith stepped onto the stage. He looked very, very young, possibly because of his bad skin. It soon became clear that the point of his act was to tell lengthy stories in a way that was deliberately unfunny.

'Albert Camus phones the Sartre household in Saint Germain des Prés and Simone de Beauvoir answers. 'Is Jean-Paul free?' asks Albert. There's a long pause, then Simone says: 'Well, up to a point."

Silence followed, then, eventually a snort. It had emanated from Gaz, and it was unclear whether it expressed amusement or derision.

'Don't see what's existentialist about this,' whispered O'Mahony to Eustace. 'Pile of shite, if you ask me.'

Kevin Smith, though, was better received by some sections of his audience. Gaz, even, was prepared to allow that his unfunniness was itself quite funny, once you got used to his technique. O'Mahony snorted at this observation, but resisted his inclination to heckle. Kevin Smith's repertoire of existentialist anecdotes lasted some ten minutes. He ended his act abruptly, leaving the stage with a curt 'Thank you' and making straight for the bar at the rear of the room. Amy appeared from behind the curtain and dutifully asked the audience to put their hands together for Kevin Smith. Some did, some didn't, Seamus O'Mahony emitting a loud whistle of mock enthusiasm.

Amy went on to introduce a succession of other acts. A very large young man took the stage with a very small young man, who pretended to be a ventriloquist's dummy. The conceit worked quite well, until the very small young man forgot his lines. O'Mahony could not resist a solitary heckle.

'Get off!' he shouted.

'Shut your face,' the very small young man returned, quick as a flash. The audience laughed uproariously.

An earnest young woman with flame red hair and a guitar that was slightly out of tune sang earnest songs about the death of Bobby Sands and the Brixton riots.

A beautiful couple dressed as if for the circus came on and juggled what looked like pieces of offal to the strains of a crackly Django Reinhardt LP.

And then it was time for the grand finale.

'Our final act this evening,' announced Amy, 'is Hanne and Hilde, who will perform for you a reverse striptease.'

Eustace had the very clear impression that most of the audience had been expecting this. It was probably why they had come. He caught himself condemning them for their shallowness before reminding himself that it was also why *he* had come.

The lights went down and the first notes of Ravel's Bolero struck up courtesy of a scratchy record on what passed for a sound system. When the lights came up again it was to reveal Hildegard and Hannelore, completely naked as promised, dancing with slow, measured movements to the music and staring into each other's eyes, surrounded by piles of clothes. Eustace became aware that his mouth had fallen open.

They danced naked with no trace of self-consciousness for a period of time that seemed to Eustace both infinite and as if it could never be long enough. The choreography seemed to him to be flawless. They had eyes only for each other, never once looking in the direction of the audience, who appeared spellbound.

Hilde was the first to begin the process of getting dressed. With a grace Eustace would never have believed possible, she pulled on a roomy pair of grey knickers while Hanne danced around her. A matching grey bra, equally generous in its proportions, was added next, Hanne gliding elegantly behind her partner to secure the strap. Hilde then watched as Hanne put on a large pair of brown knickers and matching bra.

'This is brilliant,' Eustace heard Gaz mutter. Certainly the Germans held the attention of their entire audience. They proceeded to add baggy tee-shirts, woolly tights, and finally boiler suits and suede boots. As the final bars of Bolero faded away, they sat back to back on collapsible seats, ostensibly reading copies of *Spare Rib*. The lights faded to black. Eustace was the first to applaud, joined immediately by Gaz, O'Mahony and then (it seemed) the rest of the audience. The lights came up again to reveal the Germans in their boiler suits wearing inscrutable expressions (was there really ironic amusement in there?) and looking, for the first time, into their audience. They effected a single, perfectly synchronised bow and disappeared behind the curtain. Amy stepped onto the stage, smiling sweetly.

'Thank you for coming. We hope you've enjoyed our evening of alternative cabaret. We wish you a good weekend.'

16 May

'Why didn't you tell me about it?' Eustace wondered aloud. It was the following morning and Eustace and Amy were lying in bed in her flat in Crouch End. (There was still no sex, but Eustace had once again been permitted to sleep with a hand on Amy's breast.)

'I thought Hanne would have told you, or Hilde,' said Amy. 'Anyway, I don't expect you to give me a full account every time you add a line to a poem.'

'That's different,' Eustace protested.

'I don't see how. We're both putting together a body of work. Mine exists in the moment, yours may last longer – eventually.'

"No poem is ever finished, only abandoned," quoted Eustace piously. Responses of the logical, coherent variety always eluded him when Amy spoke as if it was a given that they were both creative artists.

'Hmmm,' said Amy, unconvinced. 'I think that you're just miffed because you might have missed the chance to see two beautiful women in the buff.'

'I see them in the buff all the time!' Eustace returned. 'I mean, it's not exactly unusual, is it? What was unusual was the reverse striptease idea. Creative, subversive...'

(He realised he was quoting O'Mahony.)

'Are you quoting O'Mahony?' asked Amy.

'No,' he answered, too quickly and too loudly.

'Thought so,' she said. 'Never mind. You can write a review if you want. If you'd like to be helpful.'

'Okay,' Eustace agreed uncertainly. 'I'll think about it.'

Amy removed his hand from her breast.

'Coffee, I think,' she said, drawing the curtains open and letting in bright sunlight.

'And a Woodbine.'

The sight of her naked body framed against the day made Eustace suddenly aware of a significant erection.

'Sounds good,' he said weakly.

21 June

Suddenly, or so it seemed to Eustace Tutt, it was the longest day, and still the words refused to come. Life was tolerable, good even, when he wasn't scrubbing out a sluice or pushing a broom along a gloomy hospital corridor. Amy had indicated in a manner that was almost unequivocal that full sexual congress was in prospect (though not necessarily imminent). A spell of unexpected good weather had resulted in several trips to a little-frequented spot on

70

Hampstead Heath with Gaz and the Germans (and, on one memorable occasion, Amy) where skinny-dipping had been enthusiastically engaged in in a pond of brackish water, though not by Eustace, who had found himself curiously incapable of removing his shorts. And Gaz had gained a place at Goldsmiths. He was going to be an artist, the disappearance of the Brixton fish notwithstanding. It was official. But what of Eustace's ambitions? Lying on his front in the shade of an oak, watching his oldest friend frolicking naked in the water with Hildegard and Hannelore, Eustace Tiberius Tutt decided it was now or never. He reached for his shoulder bag, took out his notebook and pen and thought, long and hard. And when he wrote, the words suddenly came to him, faster almost than he could commit them to paper.

He had fourteen lines by the time Gaz and the Germans waded to the bank, their bodies gleaming wet in the dappled sunlight.

'What's that?' asked Gaz, catching sight of the notebook. 'The magnum opus?' Eustace put it away hurriedly. At that moment he could almost believe it just might be.

'Just a few scribbles,' he said. 'Work of genius, obviously, but just scribbles.'

'You should have come in,' Hannelore admonished him, reaching for a towel.

Eustace felt the familiar ache of desire.

'Next time,' he said, as he always did, and tried very hard not to look as the Germans dried themselves.

26 June
In the week that followed, scarcely a moment passed without Eustace thinking about his magnum opus. He was never without notebook and pen, and his work at the hospital was frequently interrupted as he put down his broom so he might add or delete a comma, or move a word from the end of one line to the start of the next. Gaz expressed the fear that he was becoming obsessive. Mrs Clout, coming

upon him staring blankly at the walls of the sluice on the renal ward, muttered darkly about time and motion studies, and threatened him with a formal appraisal.

'I'm not convinced your heart is in your work, young man,' she declared, more in sorrow than in anger. 'You might want to think about all the people out there who'd be grateful for your job and a wage packet to take home every week.'

Eustace grunted something that might (generously) have been interpreted as an apology rather than a rejection of her suggestion, and filled his bucket with water.

Later, he was lying on his bed at the squat, staring into space, when there was a knock on his door. Hannelore walked in before he had time to respond.

'Eustace,' she said, 'so you do exist. I was starting to ask myself. Where have you been all week? I've seen Rodney more than you.'

'I've been working,' Eustace explained, contemplating his bare feet, 'on a poem.'

'At last,' said Hannelore, closing the door behind her and coming into the room. 'And is it a good poem? Are you pleased with it?'

As ever, Eustace found himself more than a little disconcerted by the directness of her approach.

'Yes,' he began uncertainly, 'I think it's good. It isn't finished, though.'

'Is this it?' asked Hannelore, picking up a sheet of paper from his desk.

'Yes, but…' Eustace moved to get up, but Hannelore pushed him firmly back onto his bed.

'I'd like to read it,' she said, fixing him with a stare. 'Please.'

Eustace shrugged his shoulders and reached for a cigarette. Hannelore read in silence and said nothing for a long time.

'It's a sonnet,' said Eustace finally, 'sort of. Fourteen

lines.'

'Yes, I see that,' said Hannelore thoughtfully. 'It's very sad, but also very good. If I've understood, you would like to make love. With me. Is that right?'

Eustace stared at her stupidly.

'Would you like to go to bed with me?' she asked, as if she needed to grade her language to make him understand. Eustace considered the question; nodded dumbly.

'Okay,' she said.

'Okay?'

'No problem.' She was doing it again – the language grading thing. But could she be serious? Really?

Hannelore pulled her tee-shirt over her head, then fixed him with an intense stare.

'Eustace Tutt, I propose to give you a good seeing-to,' she declared.

Eustace had the briefest of moments to be impressed by her command of the vernacular before he was consumed by bliss.

Later, he visited Mrs Rasmussen to buy cigarettes.

'You're looking pale,' she remarked. 'You should spend more time out of doors. Enjoy the weather while it lasts.'

'I've been working,' Eustace explained.

'More poetry, I expect,' said Mrs Rasmussen, nodding knowingly. 'Poetry is a wonderful thing, but too much of it…' She left the rest unsaid.

'I'll bear that in mind,' Eustace assured her. He was finding it very hard to concentrate after the unexpected seeing-to from Hannelore.

A woman, seventy if she was a day, came in, bought a Hamlet cigar and left. Eustace raised an eyebrow.

'For her husband,' Mrs Rasmussen explained. 'She buys one for him every Friday. They're devoted to each other. A lovely couple.'

'Nice,' Eustace agreed. He felt curiously reluctant to

leave, and Mrs Rasmussen was as happy as ever to pass the time of day with him.

'Will you be watching the wedding on TV?' she asked, looking up from her newspaper.

'I didn't have you down as a royalist, Mrs R,' Eustace laughed.

'Oh, I'm not talking about that old pantomime,' she explained. 'I'm talking about Ken and Deirdre.'

'Ken and Deirdre?' Eustace's incomprehension was total.

'On *Coronation Street*,' Mrs Rasmussen explained, as if to a slow-witted child. 'It's the wedding of the year. I wouldn't miss it for the world.'

'Oh,' said Eustace.

28 July

After the event, no-one could remember whose idea it had been. Eustace was sure he hadn't suggested it and the Germans denied any responsibility. Gaz insisted he would never have contemplated anything of the sort and pointed the finger at Rodney, who, as usual, was somewhere else and not in a position to deny it.

But happen it did, all of that notwithstanding, and on the eve of the Royal Wedding and Eustace's birthday. It was a party the neighbours would talk about for months, and not in a spirit of wistful reminiscence.

It began early in the evening and petered out sometime between two and three o'clock the next morning – at a time when the heir to the throne, it must be supposed, was enjoying his last night of sleep as a bachelor.

The Germans had spent the day boiling pan after pan of chickpeas and had made industrial quantities of houmous, which guests had the choice of eating with carrots or pitta bread. That apart, there was no food except for a cake provided by a friend of Rodney's, which allegedly contained ingredients absent from the original recipe.

Hannelore and Hildegard took turns on the front door to ensure that no-one arriving without alcohol was allowed to enter, and as a result the kitchen table was soon sagging under the weight of several bottles of Woodpecker Cider, cans of Double Diamond, a solitary bottle of Blue Nun and a Party 7 that, as usual, no-one could open.

The music was loud and mostly angry, and included an impressive selection of punk albums borrowed by Gaz from any of his mates who were willing to oblige. The Adverts proved popular, as did the Slits and the Ramones, but it was the Clash that Eustace would remember best when he thought of that party: the Clash and London Calling.

A steady stream of guests arrived up until midnight, and while there were moments when the squat was heaving – rocking away in the London night like some curiously intense and single-minded dancer on a dance-floor – there seemed to be some curious chemistry whereby a number of guests detached themselves when required to ensure that episodes of discomfort were short-lived.

Amy came, together with half a dozen fellow students from the drama school (including Kevin the existentialist comedian) and her unfeasibly good-looking twin. O'Mahony was there for the duration, finally emerging to walk unsteadily back to Turnpike Lane shortly before three o'clock. It was half past five before he got home.

Mrs Rasmussen looked in briefly, tried the cake and managed a glass of Concord British wine before heading home in a mellow frame of mind, reflecting (to her surprise) that perhaps she would turn on the TV in her shop for the impending nuptials tomorrow after all.

Somewhere towards midnight, Eustace and Amy were sitting on a crate in the back yard when O'Mahony made his way unsteadily towards them.

'You wouldn't have a...?' he began hopefully. Amy, who'd also enjoyed a slice of the cake, passed him a Woodbine.

'You're a lady,' O'Mahony assured her, 'and don't let

anyone tell you otherwise.' He propped himself against the garden wall and struck a match, flinching slightly at his first draw on the unfiltered cigarette.

'Eustace,' he announced when his tobacco craving was satisfied, 'I've been reading your poem – the sonnet with the pond and the shapes and all. It's good. Really very good indeed. Sort of Arthur Rimbaud meets Philip Larkin. With a bit of Stevie Smith in there somewhere. I'd like to publish it in *Scripsi*. Next issue. What do you say?' Eustace stared at him dumbly.

'Eustace?' asked Amy. 'That's brilliant, isn't it?'

Eustace nodded.

'Welcome aboard,' said O'Mahony, slapping him on the back before stumbling away.

'Do you think he'll remember he said that?' Eustace asked Amy. 'I mean, when he's sobered up.'

'Of course he will,' she assured him. 'And if he doesn't, then I'll remind him. You've got a witness, Eustace.'

Poet. Po-et. Eustace rehearsed the word in his head. Not quite Arthur Rimbaud. Not quite published. But accepted for publication, and before he was twenty-one, if only by the narrowest of margins. Amy watched him utterly lost in his thoughts and lit a Woodbine.

29 July

It was midnight.

'Eustace?'

No response.

'Eustace Tutt?'

Eustace came to with a start.

'It's midnight. Happy birthday. Shall we go to bed? Time for something to be consummated.'

'Consummated?' Eustace had just enough wits about him to note that he was doing his mindless repetition trick again.

'Intercourse. Of the sexual variety,' she explained. 'You and me. Time to do it.'

She stubbed out the rest of her Woodbine on the wall;

led him into the house.

A little after five o'clock on the morning of his twenty-first birthday, 29 July 1981, Eustace Tutt woke up and sighed. He'd had an incredible dream. O'Mahony had told him he was a real poet and Amy Wildsmith had granted him sexual favours the like of which he had never imagined. He sighed again and rolled over.

There was a naked woman in his bed. It seemed to be Amy Wildsmith. Eustace Tutt was also naked. His head was far from clear, but the possibility began slowly to dawn on him that he had not been dreaming. Upstairs in the kitchen he could hear the sound of bottles going into a bin. The Germans clearing up after the party? The Ironic Royal Wedding Party. One thought led inexorably to another until Eustace could almost believe he was a poet and Amy Wildsmith's lover. He pressed his body against the warmth of her sleeping form, and promptly fell asleep.

A couple of hours later he found himself being shaken awake.

'Come on,' Amy was saying, 'show a leg. Or something. We've got a train to catch.'

'Train?' mumbled Eustace. (He was doing it again.)

'We can't stay in London,' Amy explained, pulling a tee-shirt over her head (not before Eustace had time to notice how perfect her small breasts were), 'not on a day like this. It's all going to be … you know … horribly monarchist. We need to get out.'

Eustace reached instinctively for his cigarettes, but Amy pulled his hand back. 'No time for that,' she admonished. 'We need to get to Charing Cross.'

'But where are we going?' asked Eustace in a tone of mild protest, but hauling himself nonetheless from the bed.

'The seaside, of course,' said Amy, now fully dressed. 'There's a train in forty minutes, so do get a move on,

Eustace Tutt.'

She rarely called him that these days. The effect, as intended, was to make him move faster.

'My head hurts,' he complained, suddenly made aware of this by his rapid movements. Amy ran a brush through her hair. The thought struck Eustace that she looked very Julie Christie in *Billy Liar* this morning. Who was she in that film? Was it Woodbine Lizzie?

'Sea air,' she said simply. 'Just the thing. Shall we go?'

They had a smoking compartment to themselves for the duration and smoked the whole journey. When the ticket collector looked in at Ashford, the air was so thick he struggled to establish how many tickets he should be inspecting.

They arrived just after mid-day and made straight for the beach. The town was strangely quiet. They ate haddock and chips on the sea wall under the watchful eye of a herring gull. After, they walked the length of the beach and round to the next bay.

'Is everyone else watching that bloody wedding?' Amy wondered aloud. They had passed no more than half a dozen people, a Labrador and a mongrel who seemed more Jack Russell than anything else.

They were nevertheless astonished to find themselves completely alone in the bay. The sun shone and the sea looked what Eustace's mother would have called *inviting*.

'Skinny dip?' Amy suggested. 'It almost seems rude not to, doesn't it?'

Eustace was about to demur, but Amy was already getting out of her clothes and, really, what was to stop him? On that glorious July day he didn't feel minded to deny her anything within his gift. He took off his tee-shirt, and Amy helpfully pulled down his shorts and underpants. Soon they were running down the beach, oblivious of the pebbles under their feet. Amy dived into the waves and swam out to sea with rapid, elegant strokes. Eustace followed in rather less elegant fashion, wondering how the sea could feel quite so cold.

When they were several hundred yards out Amy called to him.

'Look, Eustace Tutt, France. Clear as anything.'

Eustace looked out across the Channel, and there it was: the coast of France. In his state of heightened emotion this somehow seemed profoundly significant.

'Shall we just keep swimming?' Amy's voice carried across the waves.

Was she serious? Keep swimming, leave England, its royal wedding, its squat, its hospital, leave it all behind?

'All right,' he called back.

29th July 1981. On they swam, on and on, and on.

O Katia!

She must, of course, have got out of bed sometimes. But I never saw it happen once in our winter together. And when I say 'together', I should make it clear that we never actually lived together as such, though I slept on her sofa more than once.

Katia lived in an unprepossessing flat above a green-grocer's in North London. Her sole companion here was a fat white cat called Ashbery, whose domain was confined to the flat. It was rumoured that Ashbery had been fed half a tab of acid as a kitten and that this accounted for her unpredictable mood swings. Certainly her behaviour made no more sense to me than the work of the poet she took her name from.

It was quite by chance that I came to enter Katia's orbit. A friend had asked me to deliver a parcel of magazines to her flat because I lived nearby and it was likely to be several weeks before he came up to North London again. I dutifully called round one Saturday morning in early November, when the greengrocer downstairs was open for business and trade was brisk, but received no answer when I rang the bell to the flat. I tried again late afternoon, and this time the door was opened for me, presumably by remote control. I walked up the uncarpeted stairs, pausing uncertainly at the top.

'Who is it?' It was difficult to tell which of the several rooms that opened onto the landing the voice came from.

'Simon,' I said. 'With magazines. From Tom.'

'Come in,' called the voice.

I tried what seemed the most likely door. It was the kitchen. Tried another: the bathroom.

'What *are* you doing?' asked the voice impatiently. 'In *here!*'

I tried a third door, and this time was successful. I found myself in a dimly lit, very hot bedroom. Katia lay in the double bed with what looked like a fur coat around her shoulders while Ashbery sprawled across the second pillow.

'Katia?' I asked hesitantly.

'Well, I hope so,' she returned. 'And this is Ashbery. Simon Burrell, I presume.'

I confirmed my identity.

'Do sit down.'

She leaned over and tipped a pile of magazines – *Bella, Hello, The Economist, The New Yorker* and *Forum* among them – from the armchair beside the bed onto the floor. I did as I was told.

Katia was the most striking looking woman I had ever seen. She had exceptionally high cheek bones, eyes set curiously far apart and of different colours, and a mass of unruly raven black hair. To me, as a young man recently arrived from the provinces, she seemed extraordinarily exotic.

'Biscuit?'

We bonded over fig rolls. We talked for hours, our conversation ranging widely over subjects as diverse as

Roland Barthes, *Home and Away,* the respective merits of PG Tips and Typhoo, the assassination of the last Pope but several, neglected corners of Hampstead and Highgate, the notion of celebrity and the songs of Tom Waits. It was midnight when I left, and in all the time I'd been there, neither of us had eaten anything other than fig rolls, nor drunk anything. Katia had not once got out of bed, the most essential of human functions apparently not essential at all in her case.

For the next six months I was a regular visitor. I brought food and drink, sometimes flowers. We talked, flipped idly through magazines, or watched TV. Ashbery would go on occasional forages to the kitchen, but I never saw Katia go anywhere. On exceptionally cold evenings she would sometimes allow me to share the bed while we watched TV, but she always wore several layers of clothing and I was never invited to take off more than my shoes. There was never any physical contact between us, and while this seemed perfectly natural to her, I occasionally felt a sense of intense frustration.

I left town to spend the May bank holiday weekend with my mother. When I called at the flat on the Tuesday, there was no response. The greengrocer told me that Katia had gone away. He had no idea why or where she had gone, or if she would be back. She'd left in a taxi the day before with two suitcases and her fat white cat in a cat box.

We had spent Friday evening together, and it had been like any other Friday evening. No tension, no arguments. What did this mean?

I was as much in the dark as the greengrocer. I suddenly realised how little I had known her. In all our endless conversations she'd never once revealed where she was born, whether she had a family, what she'd done before she took to her bed, or why she'd taken to it. To this last, I now guessed the answer was boredom.

And the only explanation I could think of for her

disappearance now was boredom. *Ennui* had been a favourite word, often invoked in what I took to be a less than wholly serious fashion, but perhaps the reality had proved more than she could bear.

I bought a pound of Granny Smith's and headed for home. I never saw Katia again.

Truly Noble

His frustration was writ ever larger on his face as, despite every effort, he failed again and again to pay for the can of *Special Brew* he craved with every fibre of his being, while the queue at the one open check-out seemed almost to be moving backwards, and I was surely not the only observer to note something truly noble in his desperate desire not to leave the store without paying, while comprehending in no measure how the can of luke-warm 9% alcohol by volume could ever bear the weight of all that expectation and longing.

Interrogation

'Coming for a drink?'

A grey Friday evening, mid-September. I looked up from the computer screen and blinked.

'Sorry?'

'A drink. It's Friday. Nearly seven o'clock. You know, the weekend. Remember?' Guy had already put on his raincoat and was waiting impatiently by the office door.

I looked at my watch. 'I'd like to, Guy, but I've really got to put in a couple more hours on the Crabflower account.'

Guy shrugged. 'Suit yourself. I'm off to down a few Japanese beers. Have a good weekend.'

'You too.' But Guy had already gone, and I turned back to the computer screen.

I worked on without interruption, and it was nearly ten before I realised that my eyes had stopped transmitting messages to my brain. Reluctantly, I switched off the computer, picked up a thick file marked 'Crabflower' and placed it carefully in my briefcase.

Out in the street, I pulled the main door shut behind me, turning my key in the deadlock until I heard the click that satisfied me it was secure.

Shaftesbury Avenue was packed with people celebrating the arrival of the weekend. Tourists filled the overpriced steak houses, Londoners made for the cheaper pleasures of Chinatown; cinemas disgorged one audience before consuming the next. I negotiated the crowds, trying to maintain my usual pace, cursing the leisurely gait of tourists with time to kill. I turned left into Charing Cross Road, then made purposefully for Tottenham Court Road underground station.

On the Northern Line platform I was depressed to read the familiar words, 'Check destination on front of train'. Eight minutes. I stifled a sigh, took a John Le Carré novel from my briefcase and started to read.

I hadn't read more than a page when a train shunted into the station. Eight minutes had become two and, to my amazement, it was an Edgware train, which meant I wouldn't have to change at Camden Town. I moved swiftly to occupy the one available seat in the carriage, fastidiously removing an empty Coke can before sitting down. As the train pulled out of the station, bound for Goodge Street, I reopened my book.

Ten minutes later, I emerged into the dismal night at Belsize Park. I glanced at my watch. Quarter to eleven. It had been a very long evening.

My mobile trilled. I took it out of my briefcase.

'Hello?'

'Hello?'

'Who's calling?'

'Is that Rafferty?'

'This is Tim Simmons. Who's calling?'

'I can't hear you very well. Listen, I've been trying to get hold of you all evening. It's going ahead as planned. I was to tell you: the spuggies are fledged.'

'The what?'

'The spuggies are fledged. Can't tell you any more at this juncture. Glad I got hold of you, Rafferty. Good night to you now. God bless.'

The connection was broken as the speaker hung up. Perplexed, I returned the phone to my briefcase, and it was with a great sense of relief that I let myself into my flat and closed the door behind me. As I put down my briefcase, I could hear the insistent pulse of the answerphone in the living-room.

I pressed the answer and message buttons before collapsing on the sofa. I lay back with my eyes closed, waiting for the message. There was a loud click before the recording began. For a few seconds all I could hear was a high-pitched wail, as if someone was trying to tune a radio. Then I heard a gruff voice, strangely distant and indistinct.

' – sure you'll get back to me once it's all over. It'll be good to touch base. God bless, now, and don't forget the spugg –' The rest of the message was lost in a crackle of unintelligible static. Suddenly my eyes were wide open. I hadn't recognised the voice at all, and I was at a loss to make any sense of the message. I felt like a very large Scotch, but was loath to stir from my position on the sofa. All at once the world seemed a strange, unfathomable place.

Slowly, this seemed to matter less and less. Exhaustion overcame me, and I fell asleep where I lay.

I was awoken, from a dream which combined the events of the previous evening with elements of the plot of the Le Carré novel I'd been reading, by the impatient ringing of my doorbell. I came to with a start, momentarily surprised not to find myself in bed, and was halfway down the stairs before the bell rang again.

It was the postman, and I realised as I opened the door that it was much later than I had imagined.

'Too big for your letter box,' the postman explained, handing over a large envelope together with some junk mail for Mr Cohen, who lived in the flat downstairs. 'Be seeing you now.' He whistled cheerfully as he retreated down the garden path.

I closed the door, still only half-awake, and opened my mail. The envelope contained a giant birthday card. With a sudden shock I realised that today was the seventeenth. So yesterday had been the sixteenth – my birthday – and it had passed without my even noticing it. The card was brightly coloured and showed an ostrich trailing a banner which read *Guess who's 21? !!!* Opening the card I read the words *Happy Birthday, Birthday Boy!!!* Below this a number of letters, which had clearly been cut from a newspaper or magazine, had been stuck to the card, forming the message *Meet at Dr Johnson's summerhouse -T.*

T? Tara? Would Tara send a hideous card like this? Would she send me any card now, after all that had happened between us? But if it wasn't from Tara, why Dr Johnson's summerhouse? We'd always met there for our walks on Hampstead Heath, had even continued to meet on the site after the summerhouse had been razed to the ground by some arsonist. As if changing our meeting place would bring us bad luck. In the end, that had come to us anyway.

In the living-room I noticed the pile of mail I'd brought up with me the night before. I'd been too tired to open it then. Now it occurred to me that I might actually have received some cards on my birthday. I thought briefly about having a shower, shaving, putting on clean clothes; decided I'd open my post first.

There was a letter from my bank manager, urging me to consider taking out a loan. And two birthday cards. The first, from my mother in Bournemouth, contained a Halifax cheque for £10. The second, from my godfather – who I hadn't seen since I was five – wished me continued good health and happiness.

I reached for my briefcase. I had plenty of time; it was only just ten. I'd read a couple of chapters of Le Carré before cleaning myself up a bit. Then I'd have a bite to eat and drive up to the Heath. Perhaps Tara would be waiting for me on the site of Dr Johnson's summerhouse. Perhaps she wouldn't. Either way it seemed likely I'd find out who'd sent me the card, and maybe why.

It was a dismal day, damp with drizzle, and I had no difficulty in finding a parking space close to the entrance to Kenwood. As I made my way down the familiar path to where Dr Johnson's summerhouse had once stood, the hands on my Rolex showed five to one.

There were very few people about. It was not the sort of day that Tara and I would ever have chosen for one of our walks, but my instructions had been quite explicit.

I felt rather foolish pacing up and down, but at one o'clock precisely I was joined by two men. Both were improbably dressed in trench coats and balaclavas, and one of them was wearing a pair of Ray-bans despite the weather conditions.

'Come with us, please, Mr Rafferty,' said the taller of the two. I thought I detected the suggestion of a Belfast accent.

'I think there's been some – ,' I began, but was interrupted by the second man, who sounded faintly Italian.

'This way, Mr Rafferty. No arguments, please.'

Both men were substantially bigger than me, and it seemed unwise to protest further, so I allowed myself to be escorted off in the direction of Kenwood lake.

We crossed the bridge and entered the wood. Only when we came to a clearing did we stop.

'We'd like to ask you a few questions, Mr Rafferty,' said the Irish one.

'We're confident you won't object to the questions we propose to put to you,' the Italian continued. 'We're sure you'd like to help us just as much as you're able to.'

I felt a sudden chill.

'But there is one small favour we need to ask of you. Your eyes, Mr Rafferty – I'm afraid we have to blindfold you.'

By this stage it hardly occurred to me to dissent. They tied a thick black scarf around my head, then there was a long, silent moment before anything happened. I became aware of deep, rhythmic breathing very close to each of my ears. My companions were standing either side of me.

'Why did you come here, Mr Rafferty?'

'I – '

'What do you know about the Gospel Oak?'

'What happened to Simmons, Mr Rafferty?

The voices alternated in my ears with startling rapidity. It became clear to me that I was not intended to respond; that I had no answers to their questions.

'Who killed the Pope?'

'Who killed Tim Simmons?'

'When was sexual intercourse invented?'

'Who's screwing your girlfriend?'

'Who torched the summerhouse?'

'What happened to Simmons?'

'Who won the cup?'

'What do you know about Cable Street?'

'Who fledged the spuggies?'

'Who was in the summerhouse?'

'Was Simmons there?'

'Was Rafferty?'

'Who paid the driver?'

'Where are the Russians?'

'How do you take your whisky?'

'Who killed the Pope?'

'Who won the cup?'

'Who liquidated His Holiness?'

'Who swung from the bridge?'

'Where do I change for the Hammersmith and City?'

'Who killed the Pope?'
'Who is the man on the Clapham omnibus?'
'Who's at silly mid-wicket?'
'How do I get to Blackfriars Bridge?'
'Who played left back?'
'Was he left-footed?'
'Where's your girlfriend?'
'Who's she with?'
'Who's screwing her?'
'Who paid the bus driver?'
'What was the fare?'
'Mr Rafferty?'
'Mr Simmons?'

I had sunk to my knees and was conscious of the dampness of the ground for some time before I realised my tormentors had fallen silent. Light rain continued to fall.

Suddenly the blindfold was torn from my eyes. I blinked, and for a moment had difficulty in focusing on the little group that surrounded me.

Guy was there, and Tara. And several others from the office, too. My tormentors had taken off their balaclavas and stood there grinning.

'Happy birthday, Tim!' said Guy cheerfully, thumping me on the back. I noticed that his other hand was on Tara's shoulder.

'Happy birthday, Tim!' echoed the others.

But that was yesterday, I wanted to say. Instead I smiled weakly, slowly understanding everything. Almost everything.

'We thought this would be more original than a strippergram,' Guy grinned.

I looked at the smiling group around me, at Guy and Tara in their new-found intimacy, and felt a hole in my guts.

'Nice one, gang', I managed to say. 'Nice one.'

Literary Pursuits

By an effort of pure will, I succeeded in reaching the top of the escalator before she reached the bottom. I noted with relief that she was heading for the Northern Line. I might not yet be taken too far out of my way.

I walked down in a more leisurely fashion, although I was well aware of the dangers of complacency. Disaster had struck too many times before. Things would seem to be under control and then, without warning, a train would screech to a halt, she would get in, the doors close and the train pull away as I arrived, red-faced and sweating, on the platform. In my worst nightmares I still see the rear end of a tube consumed by the dark of a subterranean tunnel.

But this time I felt confident. The difficult part had been when she changed unexpectedly from the Victoria Line. I had almost been caught unawares. Isherwood had momentarily distracted me, and only by chance had I glanced up to see her getting out. I had been sure she was making for Finsbury Park, but my intuition proved defective again. I leapt from my seat and just made it out onto the platform before the doors thudded shut behind me. It was very close. I resolved to be more wary of my intuition in these matters.

She was standing below the matrix indicator, which informed me that the next train for Edgware was due in three minutes. I went and stood beside her. She was still absorbed in Virginia Woolf. I had noticed, by the ploy of pretending to tie my shoelaces when we got on at Victoria, that she was reading *Orlando*. If it had been Iris Murdoch, Katherine Mansfield or even Angela Carter, I might have turned away. But Virginia Woolf was different. Virginia made her worth the chase.

The wait for the train seemed interminable. Her clothes were exactly right. If she had consulted me about them, they would have been no different. She wore loose-fitting jeans, which, nevertheless, clutched in all the right places. And her Fair Isle sweater somehow left little to the imagination, which I both regretted and appreciated. My imagination is like a dog I am ready to exercise, yet happy for someone else to.

Her strawberry blonde hair was exactly the appropriate length and her face contained perfect measures of innocence and experience, of invitation and distance, of warmth and aloofness. She was flawless in every respect. She played the flute, I decided, and liked to paint, probably in a vaguely Pointillist manner. In her reflective moments she liked to unwind to Brahms or Schuman, while in more boisterous moods she took pleasure in shocking sensitive males by downing pints of bitter in the public bar. She was creative, charming, mysterious and alluring. She was everything I needed her to be.

She didn't get on when the train arrived. I almost said to her, *If you want the other branch, you can change at Camden Town, you know.* But I stopped myself just in time. I was sure she must have noticed my spontaneous movement towards the platform when the train came in, and I felt very awkward when I stepped back. But she seemed too absorbed in Virginia Woolf to wonder at my gauche behaviour.

That morning she had looked very different. Shorter, rounder, more solid somehow. Her hair had been jet black and spiky. She was wearing a different mask. Her morning mask was raw sensuality, while this evening mask was the sensitive aesthete's. It seemed to me now that I liked this mask better. Also, she'd been reading Elizabeth Bowen. Elizabeth couldn't compete with Virginia.

The Mill Hill East train arrived early. I moved towards the platform, but I noticed that once again Virginia hadn't moved. She was still there, like a statue almost, a waxwork from Madame Tussaud's. I stepped back towards her and was only just in time to stop myself from saying *You must want this one!* I felt perplexed and anxious. This had never happened before. We were in uncharted territory.

I was sure now that she had noticed me. My discomfort increased. She showed no sign of giving me any thought at all, but I could sense what she was feeling. Then I became aware of someone passing by on the platform. She was my height exactly, slender, with very long limbs, and wore a brown leather jacket. I could see that she was a natural blonde. I noted her Slavic features with approval. Instinctively I glanced down at her hands and was gratified to see that she was carrying a copy of *The Bell Jar*. Sylvia Plath. That would do. I hesitated, but only for a moment. Soon I was following her down the passage and up the escalator. Then disaster struck. A swarm of passengers from the Northern Line south-bound came between us and we were separated. Perspiring desperately, I raced towards the point where I had last seen her, and by an effort of pure will I succeeded in reaching the top of the escalator before she reached the bottom. I noticed with relief that she was heading for the Victoria Line. I might not yet be taken too far out of my way.

94

Open

S he sits alone in the back room, where she once served tinned soup, meat and two veg and steamed pudding to silent, solitary businessmen protected by their broadsheets, and half watches the flickering black and white images on the last analogue TV set in the neighbourhood. The shop is open for business, but with no stock for sale despite the handwritten warning: THIEVES WILL BE PROSECUTED. Her window display is a still life, executed with technical precision: two empty milk cartons, a tin of processed peas faded by sunlight, and a single lavatory roll (canary yellow).

Greenwich Village Noir

I was talking to a friend about an out of print crime novel from the sixties that I'd been trying to track down for months when she happened to mention a bookstore in Greenwich Village called 'Partners in Crime', where I might find it. She suggested visiting their website, but since I happened to be going to New York the following week on business I thought I'd check the place out for myself. It would be more satisfying to find the book on a shelf than track it down on some list on the internet. After all, this was a book I really needed to own: *The Manhattan Murders* by Irving Wohleber. As far as I knew, no-one much read Wohleber any more, but I'd discovered his work by accident while browsing in one of the bookshops in Hay-on-Wye and found his prose strangely addictive. Imagine Chandler meets Simenon and add a dash of Henry Green and you'll be somewhere near it.

I flew into JFK on a grey Saturday in late November, headed into town and checked in at my usual hotel on the Lower East Side. Normally, I'd have taken time to unpack, relax, maybe get a coffee, but today I needed to be somewhere else, and that was the Partners in Crime bookstore in Greenwich Village. Normally, I'd have walked, but such was my excitement that I hailed a cab to get me across town faster.

Partners in Crime was in one of those beautiful little streets where the trees growing on each sidewalk meet in the middle. The shop itself was below street level, an unassuming business with a discreet window display of the latest titles from Europe – England, Sweden, Iceland. I'd heard that Iceland was getting big in crime.

I hurried down the steps into the shop, barely noticing the assistant at the cash register next to the door, and made straight for the 'out of print' section at the back. I was pleased to see that the books here were not in alphabetical order: all the longer to savour the delicious uncertainty of whether I would find Wohleber's novel. I started at the bottom shelf, working my way systematically from left to right, refusing to allow myself to be distracted by the numerous beguiling titles I came across. My eyes swept the next shelf, right to left. Still no joy. On the third shelf up my heart missed a beat when I saw Wohleber's name, but it was a novel I already possessed, and in the very same edition. The fourth shelf proved something of a disappointment, and I was beginning to feel despondent by the time I'd stood up, feeling slightly dizzy, to check the top shelf. My eyes were travelling left to right again, and the excitement I felt when I saw *The Manhattan Murders*, in pristine condition, three volumes from the end, was indescribable. As slowly as I could manage, I took the book from the shelf. It was a first edition, dated June 1969, and was priced at a mere thirty dollars. The cover was a brilliant piece of period art by Jonny Fowler, depicting in graphic detail, as murder victim an improbably curvaceous blonde with a beehive hairstyle and a dagger through her heart. I closed my eyes, then opened them again to savour the excitement of my find.

Eventually, I walked to the front of the store to make my purchase.

'I'll take this,' I said, placing the book on the counter and reaching into my pocket for my wallet. The assistant did not respond. 'I've been looking for this for months,' I went on, checking my other pocket and finally locating my wallet. No response.

I looked up and saw at once that I wasn't going to get a response from this shop assistant, not today. Her hair-style was an anachronistic beehive, her waist tiny and her bosom huge. And, yes, she'd been stabbed – right through the heart. With a dagger.

Ashes

Le 27 octobre

I had been working at the *lycée* as the English *lecteur* for several weeks before Mireille spoke to me, so I was more than a little surprised when it finally happened. She was sitting in her usual chair, in the corner of the teachers' room, smoking a cigarette – *Disque Bleu* – and making a show of reading *Le Monde,* when suddenly she looked up and caught me staring at her. All at once, she assumed a knowing look, and beckoned me over. I turned round to make sure it was me she was signalling to, then crossed the room, cup and saucer in hand.

The first thing that struck me was that her English was perfect, no trace of an accent. I hadn't even known that she spoke the language at all – someone had once remarked in passing that she taught Latin and Greek.

'How do you find us here in Mainville?' she asked, looking me up and down without the slightest sign of any embarrassment.

'I like it here very much,' I replied automatically, and not entirely truthfully.

'Really?' She raised an eyebrow. 'I should have thought you would find it rather dull. Especially in the evenings.'

I sat down on the hard chair next to her. 'It's true there's not a lot to do,' I said, 'but my dissertation keeps me busy. And then I have my lessons to prepare.'

'Ah yes, your dissertation. Boris Vian, I hear, and his *romans noirs*.'

I was surprised she knew. I had only discussed this with Herr Schnell, my German counterpart, and as far as I knew he had never spoken to Mireille. I was briefly at a loss for words, and tried to hide my confusion by finishing my coffee.

'Very *noirs*, his *romans noirs*,' she went on. 'And yet life itself can be so much more so. You must come to dinner one evening. We have a flat in the old town. 16 Rue du 14 Juillet, third floor. Come tomorrow, seven for seven-thirty – isn't that what you English say?' She looked at me quizzically, drew heavily on her cigarette and turned back to *Le Monde*. I understood that I was dismissed.

Having no more classes that morning, I climbed the stairs to my quarters under the rafters on the top floor. I found an Erik Satie CD, put it on, and lay on my bed. I pondered Mireille's unexpected invitation and our brief conversation. I wondered who she had meant by 'we', and whether she had a family. She was a woman whose age was hard to determine – she could have been anything from late twenties to early forties. She was handsome rather than pretty, but with hair like Bardot and a figure to match. My appetite was whetted. I resolved to accept the invitation. There had never really been any doubt about it.

Le 28 octobre

I took care to arrive at precisely 7.09. I had dressed with studied insouciance for the occasion, but had managed to buy some flowers for my hostess en route, remembering just in time that chrysanthemums were deemed inappropriate for this purpose by the French (though I couldn't remember why). I found the address easily enough, and was relieved that there was no concierge to confront me at the front door. I rang the bell marked 'Bouffard' and was admitted at once to a gloomy hall, in which I could only just make out a narrow staircase some yards in front of me. This I climbed as far as the third floor, where an open door awaited me. I knocked and entered the apartment, not without a degree of trepidation.

'Mireille?' I called uncertainly.

'*Par ici*,' came the reply. I took my bearings from the direction of her voice and found her in a large, exquisitely furnished kitchen dominated by a vast black range. She turned as I came into the room, and I saw that she was dressed with some formality in a long black evening dress and high heels.

'Good evening, William,' she said, advancing on me with a glass of pinot noir, which she had evidently just poured. Rather haplessly I held out the flowers.

'I brought you these,' I explained unnecessarily.

'Charming,' she replied without looking at them, holding my gaze all the while. Somehow the flowers were suddenly on the table and I was holding the glass of wine and chinking glasses with Mireille, who was standing closer than any woman had ever stood to me in a social context and looking at me intently. In her heels she was exactly my height.

'Good health,' she said. 'Live long and prosper.'

'Live long and prosper,' I echoed, adding '*A la vôtre*' in a vain attempt to disguise my discomfort.

'Oh come now, that's much too formal for our little home,' she laughed, placing a hand under my chin. 'Even for an Englishman.' She allowed her hand to linger there a moment before turning back to her cooking.

'That smells good,' I remarked, recovering my breath.

'What is it? A local speciality?'

'Andouillettes,' she returned brightly. 'Pigs' bowels. Very good for the constitution. I'm sure you have a healthy appetite.'

A healthy appetite was indeed something I normally possessed, but it had never before been tested by this particular delicacy. I contrived to give the impression that news of the menu had filled me with nothing but eager anticipation.

'I certainly do,' I agreed, 'and they really do smell delicious.'

At that moment a door that I had taken for a cupboard opened, and a young woman of perhaps nineteen or twenty, wearing nothing but a towel, stepped into the kitchen from what was evidently a bathroom. She was tall, perhaps five foot eight or so, had dripping wet shoulder length fair hair, and was what the French call *gamine*.

'*Bon soir,*' she said, appraising me frankly.

'*Bon soir,*' I returned. 'William Morton.' I held out my hand and, as she held out hers, her towel slipped a little to reveal the faintest hint of the swell of her small breasts.

'Florence Bouffard.'

'My daughter,' added Mireille. 'Fresh from the shower.' She ran an affectionate hand through Florence's damp hair. Side by side they looked more like sisters than mother and daughter, though Florence was pretty where Mireille was handsome.

'*Je sors,*' said Florence over her shoulder as she left the room.

'She's always out,' Mireille confided. 'Whoever said youth was wasted on the young didn't know Florence. I suppose her father must have taught her something useful.'

'Her father?' I probed.

'Serge,' she explained, putting three plates on the table. 'He always dines alone, I'm afraid, so you probably won't meet him. The artistic temperament. Florence has it, too, *hélas.'*

We talked inconsequentially for some time while Mireille busied herself with the preparations for the meal. I was conscious that I had drunk more wine than was sensible by the time we sat down at opposite ends of the large deal table for the first course, which was *coquilles St Jacques.*

'Serge doesn't eat seafood,' Mireille told me. 'A lobster once followed him home from a party. Back in the nineties, of course.' She said this without the hint of a smile, and I was at a loss as to how to take it.

'I can see that might put you off.'

'Not to mention the consequences for the lobster.' This remark was so obviously intended to conclude our discussion of the topic that I fell silent.

Mireille smoked heavily between courses, lighting each cigarette from the stub of the last one. There were frequent long silences that seemed to bother her not at all. When the time came for our main course of andouillettes, Mireille piled a plate high with offal, potatoes and vegetables, placed it on a tray with a glass of wine, and disappeared somewhere into the bowels of the apartment to deliver Serge's dinner. When she returned, she passed me the plate of *andouillettes* and I helped myself to a modest portion. They looked good, but my experience of eating offal was limited to my mother's steak and kidney pie. Mireille put a substantially larger quantity on her plate, but took only one potato and a small helping of green beans. What I lacked in meat, on the other hand, I made up for with vegetables. Mireille stared at me as I transferred the first mouthful of offal to my mouth. I found the taste utterly disgusting, and a sudden vision of a van load of severed pigs' heads came unbidden to my mind.

'What do you think?' she asked coolly.

'Quite a strong flavour,' I managed to reply, 'but tasty,

very tasty.'

Mireille looked extremely pleased with herself, and turned her attention to her plate. She ate the offal with very obvious enthusiasm, and only when she had finished did she speak again.

'How's your work on Vian progressing?' she asked, adding – almost under her breath – 'So much sex and death.'

'Oh, rather slowly,' I said, 'but there's no great hurry. I've got all year to write it.'

'No time like the present,' she said darkly, taking my plate on which a sliver of *andouillette* still remained. I couldn't help noticing that she put this in her mouth as she moved from the table to the sink.

Cheese followed, then a rather half-hearted crème caramel. Mireille continued to smoke between courses, but I noted that she never collected her husband's plate, nor took him any cheese or dessert. When we had finished eating, she produced a bottle of cognac and, although by this time I was far from sober, I was persuaded to join her in several stiff measures. It must have been after midnight when I left. I had some difficulty in finding my way downstairs to the front door of the building – Mireille having bidden me farewell at the door of her apartment – but when I finally got there it was opened for me by Florence on her way in. I must have been very drunk indeed because she seemed to be dragging a young man along behind her. She raised an eyebrow at me and smiled sweetly, and I staggered off into the night, suddenly aching in my drunkenness with the profoundest desire I had ever known.

Le 4 novembre
In the week that followed I had very few opportunities to speak to Mireille, but became accustomed to her looking knowingly at me across the teachers' room. A week to the day since my unusual evening *chez Bouffard* I was sitting outside my favourite café in the old town drinking a *café*

crème and reading a short story by Boris when Florence appeared as if from nowhere and took a seat at my table.

'Hello,' I said, laying down my book.

'Hello yourself,' she replied, speaking, like her mother, without the slightest accent. 'I'll have a *café*. *Noir*.'

I hailed the waitress and ordered her coffee.

'You enjoyed my mother's company last week, I'm sure,' she remarked, taking a *Disque Bleu* from a packet in her bag and lighting up. 'She's extremely good company, and very attractive for her age, don't you think? She's exceptionally popular among the young men of Mainville. They appreciate her maturity and her … generosity.'

'Really?' I was, of course, wondering what the purpose of all this was.

'Oh yes. But perhaps your interest is in the less mature?'

Once again I was subjected to her appraising regard, and felt as if my every thought was written large on my face.

'How old are you?' I ventured to ask.

'Nineteen. You?'

'Twenty.'

Her coffee arrived, and we were temporarily distracted. When the waitress had left us, Florence stubbed out her cigarette in the ash tray and studied me intensely for some time. For my part, I felt extremely uncomfortable.

'You're free tomorrow evening, I expect?' she said suddenly. 'Then you can try my cooking. See how it compares to Mireille's.'

'Will Mireille be there?'

'Oh no, not on a Saturday.'

'And Serge?'

'Oh, he'll be around, I expect, but I don't suppose we'll see him. Shall we say seven for seven-thirty?'

I nodded in agreement, suddenly too startled to speak. She got up, kissed me on the cheek, and was gone before I had recovered my wits. All that remained was her untouched coffee.

Le 5 novembre

I was more than a little surprised when Florence answered the door in her bathrobe. 'Come in,' she said, barely glancing at me. I followed her into the kitchen, where – as her mother had done on my previous visit – she busied herself at the huge range.

'Hungry?' she asked after a while. I had seated myself at the kitchen table and was trying very hard not to imagine what she looked like under her robe.

'A little,' I said, hedging my bets and remembering my last visit. 'What are you cooking?'

'*Coeur de veau*,' came the reply. 'Mireille told me you're keen on offal and heart is my favourite.'

'Great,' I said feebly. 'I've never eaten hearts before.'

'Really?' She looked at me for the first time. 'I would have thought you were a man who was hungry for new experiences.'

Without consulting me, she poured a glass of pinot noir and thrust it at me. 'Cheers,' she said, chinking glasses. Despite myself, I couldn't help noticing that her robe was beginning to fall open. 'Cheers,' I returned, looking nervously at the table.

We ate seafood for starters: crab, lobster, mussels and prawns. Florence mentioned her father's pursuit by a lobster in the nineties. I feigned ignorance, and asked her if this had really happened. She appeared not to understand my question and lit a *Disque Bleu*. When we had finished our seafood, she left the room with a plate for her father, and didn't return for some considerable time. When she finally came back, she had taken off her bathrobe and dressed herself as an archetypal tart: black bra and tiny thong, suspender belt and stockings and dangerously high heels. She made no reference to this, but proceeded to turn off the lights in the kitchen and put a match to several candles. I was convinced she must hear the sound of my heart beating, so insistent was its pounding in my chest.

But she carried on as if nothing out of the ordinary were taking place, and served our calves' hearts.

'*Bon appetit,*' she said as she took her place at the table.

'*Bon appetit,*' I rejoined.

The texture of the heart in my mouth all but made me retch, but I managed to force a smile and mutter, 'Delicious. Thank you.' Florence herself smiled at this, the first time her inscrutable expression had changed all evening. As we ate, I did my best not to gaze too obviously at my eccentrically dressed hostess, but my success was limited. We briefly discussed my work on Vian, and Florence revealed herself to be surprisingly knowledgeable about both his fiction and his poetry. She expressed an especially high regard for *J'irai cracher sur vos tombes,* a particularly dark novel Vian had published under the pseudonym Vernon Sullivan. I must have appeared surprised.

'I like fiction to reflect life,' she explained, as if to someone of limited intelligence. 'Don't you?' I was spared the need to reply because she got up from the table at this point and took our plates to the sink. My eyes followed the progress of her perfectly proportioned body, and I could resist no longer. I stood up, crossed the room and, taking her buttocks in my hands, kissed her neck. She turned and pushed me gently, but firmly away.

'*Non,*' was all she said. Turning to the stove, she removed two hearts from the heavy pan where they had been cooking and transferred them to a plate. I understood that she intended to take her father his meal.

This time she was gone a good quarter of an hour. In some confusion, and in considerable doubt about what to expect next, I moved nervously around the kitchen in the faint light provided by the candles on the table. On the mantlepiece that surrounded the huge range I could make out a row of small pots, almost like miniature urns. I reached out and picked one up. The letters S B were engraved on it and, removing the lid, I discovered it contained a fine powder. I checked another: it proved to be identical in every respect except the initials carved on the outside. In all, there were eleven pots.

'*Qu'est-ce que tu fais?*' Florence had returned without a sound and I felt as if I had been discovered in the middle of some criminal act.

'Nothing,' I said, replacing the pot so hurriedly I nearly dropped it on the range. Turning, I was confronted by Florence in all her terrible beauty. She advanced on me, stared into my eyes and placed her hand on my groin with predictable results. Then her lips were on mine and her tongue was in my mouth.

What followed was the most intense melange of pain and pleasure I had ever experienced. My clothes were ripped from my body with such force that my shirt tore in several places. Florence was completely in command. She refused to allow me to remove any of her underwear until the precise moment she decreed, always holding out until I felt my longing must cause me to die or lose consciousness, or in some other unimaginable way cease to be, to feel. Finally she took me, sitting astride me on the kitchen table, her face contorted into the most extreme agony and ecstasy, eyes open, staring straight ahead. When I came, the sensation was so intense I cried out loud and sent a candle flying to the floor.

Florence took no more than a couple of seconds to compose herself before she climbed off me and disappeared into the shower. Though I wanted more than anything to follow her, I knew I would be turned away. When I had my breath back, I retrieved my clothes and got dressed, pulling on the shreds of my shirt.

It was some time before she emerged wrapped in a towel and looking exactly as she had the first time I set eyes on her.

'No dessert,' she remarked matter of factly. 'I'll get us some cognac.' She blew out the candles, turned on the lights and poured us two very substantial cognacs. For the rest of the evening there was no reference to what had happened between us. Without saying anything, Florence managed to make it perfectly clear that this was not a subject for discussion.

When I came to leave, I realised I had once again had too much to drink. Florence saw me to the door and kissed me hard on the lips.

'*A la prochaine*,' she said, with the closest she came to a smile, and closed the door.

I passed Mireille on the stairs. 'Sweet dreams,' she said, in a voice I didn't recognise as hers.

Le 6 janvier

'You must be the new *lecteur*. I'm Mireille Bouffard. Pleased to meet you.'

'Simon Harker. *Enchanté*.'

'You must come to dinner one evening. We live in the old town.'

'I'd love to.'

'Tomorrow, then. Seven for seven thirty – isn't that what you English say? 16 Rue du 14 Juillet. Third floor.'

They smiled and shook hands.

'I look forward to it,' he said.

Free Association

'Green?'

'Jealousy.'

[Long silence.]

'The time she crept downstairs in the middle of the night and checked my text messages. Nothing there, of course, but it didn't stop her dropping my phone in the loo.'

[Raised eyebrow.]

'It was back where she'd found it the next morning, more or less dried out. But it didn't work any more. Never worked again. All the evidence destroyed.'

'Evidence?'

'Well, what she saw as evidence. And without the actual texts she could, you know, make the words do whatever she wanted them to.'

'Which was?'

'Make it look as though I was the one who'd been carrying on, when in fact it was her. She'd been seeing someone else.'

'She admitted this?'

'Yes. No. Well, not in so many words. But I saw the texts.'

'Texts?'

'On her phone.'

'You checked her text messages?'

'No. Yes. I knew something was going on.'

'So you confronted her?'

'Yes, I confronted her.'

'And?'

'She denied everything. Said I was paranoid, shouldn't have been looking at her messages. I was reading things into them, apparently.'

'Were you?'

'No. It was there, in black and white.'

'Like your texts?'

[Pause.]

'What do you mean?'

'Didn't she think your texts were evidence?'

'But they weren't.'

'No?'

'No. No. I mean ... no.'

[Silence.]

'Is it conceivable that neither of you were, so to speak, carrying on?'

'What are you suggesting?'

'Is it possible that neither of you were ... guilty as charged?'

'I saw her texts.'

'She saw yours.'

[Very long silence.]

'Yellow?'

'Custard.'

The Woman Who Liked to Run

The woman who liked to run liked to run for all manner of reasons. Firstly, she had discovered, rather late in life, it must be conceded, that she ran very well. She could run long distances without tiring, and quickly developed the habit of running anything up to fifteen miles over the Mendips before breakfast. Secondly, exercise on this scale kept her in the kind of shape that was much admired by many men and not a few women and, while this wasn't (of course) a primary consideration, it didn't displease her that heads turned with extraordinary (some might have said tedious) predictability whenever she ran past in her Lycra shorts and a vest that revealed a good six inches of very flat stomach. And thirdly, running provided her with an opportunity to escape for a while all the demands of running a household of four children, none of them yet in their teens, a Jack Russell puppy who was proving to be untrainable in any meaningful sense of the term, and two parrots. The childrens' nanny, whose presence in the house allowed – or could be deemed to allow – her early morning runs, was not herself a morning person and rarely appeared until after the woman who liked to run had returned and showered. Increasingly, she was not an afternoon or evening person either, and as a result the woman who liked to run found she had more and more reason to run, and more and more to run from. These were some of the things she had to run from: the untrainable puppy, who had no interest in defecating outdoors, invariably depositing pungent brown turds at strategic intervals around the kitchen during the night, the cleaning up of which was no way for the woman who liked to run to start her days; the nanny – whose name was Elspeth but liked to be called 'Els' – who interpreted her brief in the very narrowest of terms and was at pains not to be accused of any excess of zeal; while her children – well, they were just too many. As to the absence of any man about the house, the less said the better. And as to the challenges presented by two garrulous parrots who very definitely did not get on – ditto.

The woman who liked to run had run at least seven and a half miles one morning in early January – at which point it was her habit to turn back with thoughts of a hot shower and a bowl of muesli – when something happened. She was not, of course, remotely tired. Two male dog-walkers had paused to sneak a rear view as she passed them (one late thirties, handsome in an obvious kind of way, with a retriever; the other sixties, short and grumpy-looking, with some kind of mongrel), which had not gone unnoticed. And she was feeling a sense of joy, a sense that increased in direct proportion to the distance between her body and her home.

On she ran, the wind in her auburn hair.

Cocktail Party

Nice party.
    Hmm.
    You a friend of Bill's?
Margaret's. You?
Colleague. Of Bill's.
At the ad agency?
Uh huh.
Oh.
How do you know Margaret?
College. Well, uni.
Oxford?
Edinburgh. We did our doctorates together.
That's nice. You've known each other a good while, then.
Kind of. There was a long ... interval. We only hooked up again recently. Facebook, you know. You and Bill?
Sorry?
Known each other long?
No, not long, no. Couple of years maybe.

Oh.
Live near here?
No. Used to.
Really? Me too. Next street.
Athelston?
Marshall Terrace.
Really? That's a coincidence. I used to live there myself.
Sorry, I didn't introduce myself – Dominic.
Davina.
Davina? Didn't we used to be...?
Married?
To each other?
No, I don't think so.
Oh. Cashew?
No thanks. Yes, nice party.

Chaos Theory on a Bad Gravy Day

I f she hadn't burned the gravy, he wouldn't have felt obliged to tell her how much he'd always hated the way she made it. She might never have known that it was his considered opinion that she overdid the flour and had no intuitive sense of the appropriate moment to stop adding stock. She wouldn't, therefore, have felt the need to confide in him how much she had always resented his flatulence about the house, nor complain that this increased her distaste for the business of washing his Y-fronts. He, in turn, would surely not have mentioned his own distaste at her fondness for short skirts, a fondness that, in his judgement, was not altogether seemly in a woman approaching the menopause, actually. And if he hadn't mentioned that, she would surely not have felt that it was only fair to point out that it might be considered less than seemly for a man of his age to wear his hair so long and his trousers so tight. In which case, he would not have said that it was pathetic of her to resent him for achieving a better class of degree than her, and she would not then have countered that nobody in their right mind would want *any* class of degree from the university he had attended. He wouldn't have suggested that she was turning into her mother, nor would she have responded that, in point of fact, *he* was turning into *his* mother (and also his great aunt on his father's side). And if all that hadn't come to pass, she probably wouldn't have ended up pouring the offending gravy over his head and he wouldn't have assaulted her with an organic parsnip.

Hell, they might still be married! Hell, the Twin Towers might still be standing.

Dance Me to the End of Love

You'd have been fifty today. Strange thought. If either of us was going to die young, most people would have bet on me. Perhaps that's why most gamblers are losers.

When I close my eyes I see you at twelve, at eighteen, at thirty. But if I keep them closed long enough – and I often do – I see you at forty. In bed, unable to speak, unable to move. Always with the faint stench of piss about the place, despite the best efforts of the staff. And I'm sure they did their best. But you lay there day after day, week after week, month after month. Year after year. Until you slipped quietly away, and it felt as if you'd been somehow extinguished.

We are seventeen and the world is fresh, exciting. We're discovering music, books, art. We both decide we're going to be writers. What else would we be? Fitzgerald is your man, Camus mine. But we read whatever we can find and discuss earnestly. There are others in our class who read,

I remember, and Dos Passos. Fitzgerald, of course, and Steinbeck. When I'm not swimming, I read Camus, everything I can find, by and about. Toy with the idea of going in goal next time we play football. There must be stuff to be learned from going in goal if Camus was a goalkeeper.

One morning, early September, I'm on the beach alone for once, soon after nine, reading *L'Etranger* again. I look up and see a vision emerging from the sea. She shakes her sopping dark brown hair, which hangs like seaweed as she stands in the shallows, oblivious to everything but the moment. I realise it is Sara. We are no more than thirty yards apart and I mean to call out to her, but I can't. No words come. I feel the blood rush between my legs and am immediately ashamed that this is my response to what I see: Sara, more beautiful than ever, salt water glistening on every inch of that perfect body.

And suddenly it's too late. And in any case I'm too embarrassed by the swelling in my shorts. Sara hasn't noticed me, and is walking up the shingle in the opposite direction. I realise we're not alone on the beach, despite the early hour. There are at least a dozen others, and a dog. An elderly golden retriever. I roll onto my front, try to concentrate on my book.

Your grades are better than mine. You go to the university you'd set your heart on, no more than fifty miles away. I go to my second choice in a grey city in the Midlands. We write, long, long letters, at least once a week, sometimes more. I think about writing to Sara, but never quite do.

That Christmas, we're both back in our home town. We're walking along the cliffs on the first Monday of the vacation when you tell me you're seeing Sara, have been seeing her since the start of term more or less. She's been to stay with you and you've been back to the coastal town to see her. And you *have* written letters to her, and she's written letters back to you. But there was no mention of this in your letters to me. And how did you know it would matter so much, when I had no idea? How could you have known that? I'm staring out to sea. Pale Arctic sun on waves. You're still talking, but all I can hear is words that don't mean anything. As if you're speaking Hindi or Malay. And when I finally turn to look at you, I'm so incensed that I start to push you, closer and closer to the edge of the cliff. You don't resist. In my memory, we're inches away from disaster when I stop, give you a long look and turn away. In reality, we were probably nowhere near. But the sensation of having been kicked in the guts, that was real enough. All the more real because you hated violence so intensely.

We don't speak again until Christmas Eve. Everyone's back from university by now and we all congregate in the usual place, the Gardener's Arms. We avoid each other carefully until we've drunk too much to sustain the distance between us any longer. Awkward at first, then, as our conversation progresses down familiar paths, less so and less so until we're standing outside the pub and hugging each other as if nothing ever happened. I walk home, back to the terraced house at the other end of town, back to number 21, and meet my parents returning from midnight mass at the front door. They pretend not to notice that I've drunk too much, and we exchange Christmas greetings. The house already smells of roast turkey, the bird roasted on Christmas Eve so the day itself can be a more relaxed affair. That's their theory.

In my bedroom, I feel suddenly compelled to hunt through the drawer of my desk for a photograph. It takes a while, but I find it. The only photograph taken of me and Sara while we were together, black and white, taken on Good Friday. We're sitting on the harbour wall and it must be quite cold. I'm in a duffle coat, she's in a suede jacket and wearing a beret. We're both laughing at the camera. And through the fog induced by exhaustion and too much beer, and the emotion of the evening in the pub with everyone back together for the first time since we all went away, I torture myself trying to remember who took that photograph. Was it you? *Was it you?* I wake up cold but still fully clothed a few minutes after seven on Christmas morning.

After that Christmas vacation we don't see each other for six months. I don't remember why. Perhaps we're both enjoying student life too much. By the time we meet up in the summer, it's all over between you and Sara, and you're wondering what it was all about. I could tell you, of course, but I don't. Too much strange, unexplained pain still for that. We both have summer jobs, but see a lot of each other in the evenings and at weekends. We discuss books again, play the occasional game of tennis, go to see films at the local fleapit. Late September we're in an Indian restaurant having a curry when Sara walks in.

I'm shocked by how much she's grown up. She's a woman now, and the person she's with is a man, older and so much more sophisticated than you or me. She sees us, calls a greeting, but none of us knows what to do next. I raise a hand, an awkward gesture that leaves me feeling strangely uncomfortable. You say something incomprehensible in a low voice. Sara gives a barely perceptible shrug as she and her companion are ushered to a table at the other end of the restaurant. You ask for our bill. When we leave, I notice that your side dish has been left untouched.

We lived so intensely then, or convinced ourselves we did. We really believed we had a duty to use ourselves up, burn ourselves out. If God was dead, what else was there? Then somehow, suddenly we got to be forty. Things happened, of course, in the intervening years, but they didn't happen with the same intensity. We graduated, got jobs, to avoid any direct acknowledgement of what we both knew: that you would soon be gone. It was autumn, a glorious autumn day, leaves all around our feet, and the trees every shade of red and brown. I remember how it felt like something ending.

And ten days later at the crematorium. The Humanist funeral you would have wanted, if you'd been able to tell us: God shut out. Rachel's brother playing a Paul Simon song on his guitar, me reading from Dylan Thomas. Those timeless lines. And what I remember most: a sudden compulsion to turn round. The sight of Sara in the back row. Our eyes meeting. How had I known?

That night, I didn't drive back to London as planned. Sara and I met at the Gardener's Arms, as we'd met there on so many occasions thirty years before. We drank very little, turned down a glass for you, and hardly spoke. I remember thinking: she has become her mother, she has her mother's grace.

United by our broken marriages, we walked to the house where Sara now lived alone. A tall, thin terraced house with huge rooms, high ceilings. In her sitting room I recognised one of her father's landscapes on the wall above the fireplace: Sutherland, perhaps, or Caithness.

Sara lit a fire in the grate, candles on the mantelpiece. I was touched to see a stack of LPs and a record player with a turntable. No sign of any CDs. I flicked through the records. The Beatles, Van Morrison, Joni Mitchell, Leonard Cohen. Leonard Cohen. Carefully I took the record from the sleeve, placed it on the turntable, and hesitantly moved the arm with its stylus onto the disc.

The strains of 'Dance Me to the End of Love' filled the room.

'Sorry,' I said. 'Corny, I know.'

Sara smiled, looking more than ever like my memory of her mother.

'Fuck corny,' she said, and all I could think was that

was the first time I'd ever heard her swear, in all those years. And so what had failed to happen thirty years before happened there, then, in that sitting room on a rug in front of a smouldering fire, corny or not. Sara danced me to the end of love.

You'd have been fifty today. Midsummer's day. What you would have made of me and Sara, and the story of how your death brought us together again, I can't begin to imagine. But from some unfathomable source those words of Fitzgerald's you used to be so fond of quoting surface, and repeat themselves again and again in my head:

'So we beat on, boats against the current, borne back ceaselessly into the past.'

Indeed we do. We *are*.

The Numbers

Night after night this was how they sat. She, as if at prayer, listening to the wireless. He, hunched over his newspaper, engaged in comprehensive study, working his way from the back pages to the front, not because affairs of state were less important than the football results, just because they would wait.

Between them? A sideboard, with vase and mirror, and the delicious lack of any need to talk. But at nine o'clock he would look up, raise an eyebrow and she would give the faintest nod of her head. One and one for two: a cup of tea (small) and a slice of buttered toast (small), served no more than ten minutes later. Eaten in companionable silence, wireless muted. And then to a discussion of the day, perhaps a brief flirtation with the prospects for tomorrow.

And how many evenings unfolded in this way? More than either of them could say, or would ever have believed. From evenings that were January coloured through to evenings that were December tinted, and back again.

And then there was one. No newspaper now, just the

wireless. And at nine, different hands that made the tea, buttered the toast. One and one for one. But still she spoke of the day, flirted with the prospects for tomorrow. Until there was no tomorrow.

And when they came to clear the house, they found that two chairs were heavier, were just a little harder to move, than they had any business being. Almost as if they had become one with the house's foundations. And in the room, a strange, comfortable silence. Companionable, you might have said.

Правда (*Pravda*)

Then I went back into the house and wrote, It is midnight. The rain is beating on the windows. It was not midnight. It was not raining.
Samuel Beckett

'Take *pravda*,' said Hilary.
'*Pravda*?'
'As a case in point.'

Hilary Broughton, Professor of Language Death Studies, and Jasper Clough, Professor of Life Science, had climbed the mound that overlooked the university campus, and were both slightly out of breath.

'Isn't it the name of a Russian newspaper?

Hilary gazed out across the campus. Below them several hundred students went about their business, studying, drinking coffee, discussing matters weighty and insubstantial, sleeping, making various versions of love, indulging in the odd spliff.

'Russian perhaps,' said Hilary. 'I'll concede that.

'Newspaper' is more problematic. On the face of it, *pravda* is the Russian word for truth. Or perhaps more accurately the *Russian* for truth. But what truth? Whose truth?'

Spring had arrived after a long, grey, wet winter, and the Downs had rarely looked so pleasing, or so it might have seemed to Jasper, had he given it any thought. Hilary took a tin of tobacco from the pocket of his tweed jacket and set about rolling himself a cigarette.

'When the Soviet tanks rolled into Czechoslovakia in 1968, the 'truth' was proclaimed as the quelling of a fascist uprising,' Hilary continued, 'and as soon as a word like '*pravda*' or 'truth' can be made to comfortably accommodate its own opposite – an act of the purest linguicide, I would contend – we must see the processes of language change as so advanced that language death becomes inevitable. And by 'language death', I mean, of course, the death of all language and all languages.'

He struck a match and lit his cigarette. As usual, it was beautifully rolled. Jasper surveyed the undulating downland.

'I see,' he said, taking a packet of mints from his tweed jacket. His breathing had, by now, returned to normal, unlike Hilary's, which was still a little laboured. 'So language change is a necessary condition for language death,' he went on tentatively, putting a mint in his mouth.

'The timeframe is impossible to predict,' said Hilary, 'because language has never before been subjected to the pressures it faces today: the internet, 24 hour news, celebrity culture, social media, politicians, management gurus – all doing their damnedest without even realising it. But yes, eventually language change will sow the seeds of language death.'

'But we won't live to see it,' Jasper suggested hopefully.

'Oh, we'll see language death all right,' Hilary returned, carefully stubbing out the butt of his roll-up. 'It's happening all the time. But it isn't language change that's causing it yet. We're a few centuries away from Armageddon.'

Jasper sucked thoughtfully.

'Shall we go down?'

Facts: 3,176 languages are officially endangered. 9.2% of living languages have fewer than ten speakers. 639 languages that once existed are extinct.

'Come!' called Hilary at her first knock.

The door opened a little and her head appeared.

'Sorry?'

'Come, come,' Hilary repeated.

'In?' she asked.

'Yes, in.' This with a hint of impatience. 'Come in.'

The ritual complete, Eleanor entered, closing the door firmly behind her. Six foot in her stockinged feet – though today she was stockingless – with auburn hair scraped into a bun whose continued existence looked precarious at best. The faux NHS spectacles. Today she was wearing a green cotton mini-dress and – apparently – very little else. Hilary considered her carefully.

'Sit!'

Eleanor held his gaze as she seated herself in an armchair by the window. Hilary rose from his desk, determined not to be distracted – yet – by the thigh she had artfully crossed over its partner for his edification.

'Progress?' he asked.

'Some.'

He loved the way she said that: her Cornish accent just discernible, if you knew what you were listening for. Which Hilary, naturally, did.

'Hmm.'

He reminded himself of the facts. She was considerably less than half his age. He was a married man, who'd loved his wife Dorothy, a librarian, for many years. They had two children, now grown up, and a beagle/cocker spaniel cross. They took their holidays in Italy, Umbria one year,

Tuscany the next. They lived in a comfortable detached house with a large, well-tended garden. He was Professor of Language Death Studies at the University of the South Downs. She was his doctoral student, researching the evolution of Cornish and the prospects for Kernewek Kemmyn in the twenty-first century. They had been involved in an intimate relationship, which she had initiated, for more than two years. He was a married man. She was his doctoral student. His house was detached. His wife was a librarian. He loved his wife. He would always love his wife. Dorothy – that was it, Dorothy. Would it be Tuscany or Umbria this summer? The children were grown up. The dog was a beagle/cocker cross. The dog was called Barney. Barney was fluent in both Cornish dialects. Eleanor was his grown-up child. Green was the colour of truth. The garden was well-tended. The garden was the colour of truth.

Hilary cleared his throat.

'Anything else?'

She shook her head and her hair fell loose. Auburn was the colour of truth. She pointed to the window.

'Blinds' she commanded.

Hilary closed the blinds.

'More light,' she commanded.

Hilary obliged.

Eleanor pointed to the door.

'Lock,' she commanded.

Hilary locked the door. Eleanor stood, removed her spectacles and placed them carefully on Hilary's desk. Then, grasping the hem of her dress, she pulled it up over her head and threw it into a corner. She stood before him in her unstockinged feet, enjoying the helplessness in his eyes before advancing on him.

'I love you, Hilary.'

Those monophthongs! How he adored them.

'I love you, Eleanor.'

Dorothy was his wife. Barney was his dog. It would be Tuscany or, possibly, Umbria. The children were grown up. Green was the colour of truth. Or auburn was. The Russians invaded in 1968. Dorothy was a librarian.

Hilary felt breathless. He loosened his tie.

Fact: Tevfic Esenç (Ubykh), Red Thundercloud (Catawba Sioux), Roscinda Nolasquez (Cupeño), Laura Somersal (Wappo), Ned Maddrell (Manx) and Arthur Bennett (Mbabaram) were the last known speakers of their respective languages.

'The Vice-Chancellor will see you now.'

Hilary looked crossly at his watch. It was just before six o'clock, and he had been summoned for five. It had been an uncomfortable wait.

The Vice-Chancellor was seated behind his desk, a huge walnut affair.

'Hilary!' The greeting might almost have been taken for warm and welcoming.

'Vice-Chancellor,' Hilary returned warily.

The Vice-Chancellor gestured vaguely at a seat across the desk from his own. Hilary sat.

'Drink?'

Hilary declined politely, then regretted it, before he had finished explaining why not.

'How's Doris?'

'Dorothy. She's very well, thank you, Vice-Chancellor.'

'Splendid, splendid. And your research?'

'Keeping me busy, you know. Languages will keep on changing and dying.' He chuckled mirthlessly.

'Quite.'

They sat in silence for some time, Hilary aware he was being contemplated.

'You know,' said the Vice-Chancellor finally, 'there comes a time when the groves of academe begin to lose their allure. Oh, it can be a very gradual thing, usually is. We find ourselves … distracted. Struggle to maintain our focus on what it is we're here for. Do you follow?'

My house is detached, my wife is a librarian, my dog is a beagle/cocker cross. I love my wife. I take my holidays in Tuscany and Umbria. My mouth is very dry.

Hilary nodded, almost imperceptibly.

'These are challenging times for higher education, Hilary,' the Vice-Chancellor went on. 'We all need to be at the top of our game, alert to reputational issues. Take our eye off the ball and the game is lost, do you see?'

Hilary wasn't sure that he did.

'No room in the team for anyone who's going to drop the ball. No place for anyone who isn't completely focussed on goal. Going forward.'

'I see.'

It was, by now, quite dark in the room, or so it seemed to Hilary.

'A young man's game, Hilary. A brave new world. The days when a senior academic could allow himself to be distracted by the tantalising prospect of appetising young flesh are gone. Scandal is the worst kind of distraction, Hilary. We don't want it and we don't need it.'

'I see.'

'I knew you would. Look, you've had a good innings, spent longer at the crease than most. Now you've been bowled a googly and got yourself caught at square leg. It happens. There's no shame in it. Well, not much. But it's time for the pavilion steps.'

I love my wife. Barney is my dog. Eleanor is from Cornwall. My mouth is very dry. I am Professor of Language Death Studies. I am short of breath. Green is the colour of truth. The Soviet tanks went in in 1968.

'Of course, we'll have no problem with an *emeritus* for you,' the Vice-Chancellor continued. 'And you can have your name on the door of a shared office if you wish. Though it might be wise if your visits to the campus weren't too frequent – much as we'd all love to see you.'

Hilary nodded.

'Persephone has your letter. You may wish to sign it on the way out. *If it were done when 'tis done, then 'twere well it were done swiftly* ... and all that.'

'*Quickly,*' murmured Hilary under his breath. "*Twere well it were done quickly.*'

The Vice-Chancellor rose. He was a very small man, but he seemed to Hilary a long way away across the vastness of the walnut desk.

'Good-bye, Hilary. I've enjoyed our little chat. I couldn't be happier for you.'

He held out a hand. Hilary shook it limply.

Fact: Every time a language dies, a grain of truth dies with it.

'It was masterful,' said Hilary, rolling a cigarette. He and Jasper once again found themselves at the top of the mound, looking down on the campus. 'A load of nonsense about the groves of academe and people with their eyes on the ball, off the ball, bowling googlies, sticky wickets. Time to head for the pavilion. Every word an unnecessary stain on silence and nothingness, as Beckett might have said.'

'Blimey.'

'Complete and utter guff. Vacuous drivel. By the time he'd finished I could almost see a man in a white coat holding up his finger.'

'So that's it? You're going?'

Hilary lit his roll-up.

'Looks like it. I signed. The Professor of Language Death signs his own death warrant. Or as good as. Slain by cliché. Dismissed by the force of platitude. The brutal divorce of language and meaning.'

Hilary lit up.

'Have you told Dorothy?' Jasper wondered.

'Dorothy can't know the truth,' said Hilary. 'She mustn't. Gardening leave, research leave – where's the difference? Mere semantics. I may have to take myself off to Cornwall for a while. Let things blow over.'

'Cornwall? Is that wise, Hilary?'

'I'm not sure it would be wise,' Hilary returned thoughtfully, 'but in the light of my professional interests, I'd say it has the ring of truth about it. Wouldn't you?'

Jasper sucked on his mint.

Facts: In 2010 UNESCO declared that its former classification of Cornish as 'extinct' was no longer accurate. It had ceased to be extinct. 557 people claimed Cornish as their main language in the 2011 census.

The ingredients of Jasper's mint included sugar, glucose syrup, modified starch, stearic acid and mint oils.

Hilary's tweed jacket was made by hand in Donegal in 1997 and purchased from a draper in Killybegs.

I don't write a single word without saying to myself, 'It's a lie!'
Samuel Beckett

Acknowledgements

Some of these stories have been published in: *Ambit*; *BSJ: The B S Johnson Journal*; *Citizen 32*; *The Frogmore Papers*; *The Interpreter's House*; *newleaf* (Bremen).

Cultured Llama Publishing
Poems | Stories | Curious Things

Cultured Llama was born in a converted stable. This creature of humble birth drank greedily from the creative source of the poets, writers, artists and musicians that visited, and soon the llama fulfilled the destiny of its given name. Cultured Llama aspires to quality from the first creative thought through to the finished product.

www.culturedllama.co.uk

Also published by Cultured Llama

Poetry

The Other Guernica: Poems Inspired by Spanish Art by Derek Sellen
Paperback; 98pp; 203×127mm; 978-0-9957381-2-6; July 2018

Family Likeness by Michael Curtis
Paperback; 90pp; 203×127mm; 978-1-9164128-0-4; September 2018

Short stories

Canterbury Tales on a Cockcrow Morning by Maggie Harris
Paperback; 138pp; 203×127mm; 978-0-9568921-6-4; September 2012

As Long as it Takes by Maria C. McCarthy
Paperback; 168pp; 203×127mm; 978-0-9926485-1-0; February 2014

In Margate by Lunchtime by Maggie Harris
Paperback; 204pp; 203×127mm; 978-0-9926485-3-4; February 2015

The Lost of Syros by Emma Timpany
Paperback; 128pp; 203×127mm; 978-0-9932119-2-8; July 2015

Only the Visible Can Vanish by Anna Maconochie
Paperback; 158pp; 203×127mm; 978-0-9932119-9-7; September 2016

Who Killed Emil Kreisler? by Nigel Jarrett
Paperback; 208pp; 203×127mm; 978-0-9568921-1-9; November 2016

A Short History of Synchronised Breathing and other stories by Vanessa Gebbie
Paperback; 132pp; 203×127mm; 978-0-9568921-2-6; February 2017

In the Wild Wood by Frances Gapper
Paperback; 212pp; 203×127mm; 978-0-9957381-6-4; June 2017

A Witness of Waxwings by Alison Lock
Paperback; 128pp; 203×127mm; 978-0-9957381-5-7; December 2017

Dip Flash by Jonathan Pinnock
Paperback; 154pp; 203×127mm; 978-0-9957381-7-1; March 2018

Unusual Places by Louise Tondeur
Paperback; 174pp; 203×127mm; 978-0-9957381-9-5; August 2018

Curious things

Digging Up Paradise: Potatoes, People and Poetry in the Garden of England by Sarah Salway
Paperback; 164pp; 203×203mm; 76 colour illus.; 978-0-9926485-6-5; June 2014

Punk Rock People Management: A No-Nonsense Guide to Hiring, Inspiring and Firing Staff by Peter Cook
Paperback; 40pp; 210×148mm; 978-0-9932119-0-4; February 2015

Do it Yourself: A History of Music in Medway by Stephen H. Morris
Paperback; 504pp; 229×152mm; 978-0-9926485-2-7; April 2015

The Music of Business: Business Excellence Fused with Music by Peter Cook Paperback;
318pp; 210×148mm; 978-0-9932119-1-1; May 2015

The Hungry Writer by Lynne Rees
Paperback; 246pp; 244×170mm; 57 colour illus.; 978-0-9932119-3-5; September 2015

Solid Mental Grace: Listening to the Music of Yes by Simon Barrow
Paperback; 232pp; 210×148mm; 978-0-9957381-8-8; March 2018